Moment of Menace

The lustrous braid lay across his palm like a live thing, damp, soft, thick, heavy. He closed his hand. The hair was so thick that even at the end his fingers barely reached around. Suddenly and overwhelmingly he wanted to yank hard on this silky rope, to pull it back and down with all his strength. Unaware of what he was doing, he slid his hand toward her skull and the root of the braid, and his grip tightened.

A picture came into his mind of how she'd look as he held her captive like that—her face up to the sky and the front of her slim throat exposed. In the picture her mouth was open and she was screaming.

We will send you a free catalog on request. Any titles not in your local book store can be purchased by mail. Send the price of the book plus 50¢ shipping charge to Tower Books, P.O. Box 270, Norwalk, Connecticut 06852.

Titles currently in print are available for industrial and sales promotion at reduced rates. Address inquiries to Tower Publications, Inc., Two Park Avenue, New York, New York 10016, Attention: Premium Sales Department.

Concerto in the Key of Death

Barbara Fried

TOWER BOOKS NEW YORK CITY

A TOWER BOOK

Published by

Tower Publications, Inc.
Two Park Avenue
New York, N.Y. 10016

1

That's one for sure, Martin thought. I don't know how they all find their way to Roundmount sooner or later, but they sure do.

This one was a tall thin woman wrapped in batik. She also wore a long necklace of carved wooden beads, a pair of sandals whose leather straps wrapped halfway up her skinny calves before ending in great knobs of fringe, and a bunch of wilted daisies pushed into an untidy bun. She moved over to the shoulder of the dirt road and beckoned for him to pass, sweeping her bony freckled arm up from the shoulder in a cheerfully heroic, spear-waving gesture, her beads, her hair, the daisies, her batik, oscillating around her frame like sections of a mobile. As Martin ground past her in first, the tires slipping on the stones that lined the ruts, two Great Danes as bony and thin as their mistress came barking out of the leafless underbrush, and rushed at his car.

"Wouldn't you know?" Martin said under his breath. His tolerance for domesticated animals was barely greater than his dislike for their owners. "If she thinks she needs protecting, she's mistaken." Out loud he managed, "Thank you," which she acknowledged by a gracious nod before she strode off down hill, the dogs cantering stiff-legged after her, dust curling around their tawny legs.

Martin shifted into low gear. The forest had long ago coiled itself completely over and around the mountain, and an oppressive chill dimness with which he'd come to be very familiar stretched about him. The almost perpendicular road was like a narrow steep tunnel, walled by tree trunks and roofed by branches, and it was not much changed from the cart track that had been originally carved out of the woods by the Puritan settlers two hundred years earlier. They'd invested the effort then because the peak of the hill had been flattened by weathering to a gentle curve and the land there could be used. After, of course, they'd cleared it of trees and rocks.

Eventually the tunnel widened, the road leveled, the grayness lifted, and Martin drove out on top of the hill. The air was still cool, but the contrast between the forest and the open meadow was like the difference between early spring and summer. Nothing was stirring. The white-painted buildings scattered in the fields around the big Victorian main house looked abandoned and untended. Actually, Martin knew, they were empty, waiting to be filled with Roundmount's students and faculty, most of whom wouldn't be there for at least another two weeks. "Spend a creative summer in the heart of old New England," the ad read. "Roundmount. A total environment for workshops in music, art, crafts, writing, theater. Hiking, swimming, riding. For adults eighteen to eighty. Entire program under the direction of Miranda Boardman."

He pulled off the paved road onto the grassy track that went past the fieldstone dining hall, got out of the car, and ran up the shallow stone steps, across the flagstone terrace, and into the dining room, pulling the screen door with its curled spring lock shut behind him. "Anybody here?" he called. "Miranda? Are you here?" The raftered and paneled room was empty, the dozen maple tables bare. He walked through to the deserted kitchen, out the back door, around the building through the field grass, past the music barn, and back to his car. He drove a couple of hundred yards further up to the main house, went in, and searched through the downstairs. No one. He went out to the back porch and saw Miranda lugging a bucket down the path past the kitchen garden.

"Mandy! How are you? I've come early this year."

"Martin! Why, what a nice surprise." She put the pail down and held out her hands—strong, handsome, and very dirty. "How have you been? I haven't heard from you in such a long time I was beginning to think you'd given us up altogether."

"Don't be absurd," he said. "You know I'd never do that." He forced himself to touch her hands, then bent to let her kiss his cheek. She smelled of dirt and—he sniffed—yes, manure. "What in the world have you been doing? You're—you're filthy."

She stepped back. "Am I?" she said, and looked vaguely down at the front of her blouse. "I've been digging in the old river bed in the top pasture. I found a wonderful clay deposit there. A lot of the bank got washed out this spring, that's how I happened to see it. I'm about to wedge some to see if it's worth throwing and firing. Come to the potting shed, I want to show you my new electric wheel. Two speeds and everything."

"Here, let me carry that."

"No, that's all right, it's heavy. Besides, you'll get filthy yourself." She picked up the bucket and he tagged after her down the path to one of the old outbuildings, originally a stable, then a garage, and now a sculpture studio. Half the double door was open, and the sun lay across the pitted cement floor in a pale yellow rectangle, barely outshining the fluorescent light inside. Miranda set the bucket down on the ramp outside the door. An attractive redhaired woman in her late twenties was

7

sitting at the rough plank worktable sketching on a pad.

"Janice," Miranda said, "may I present a neighbor of ours, Dr. Martin Andrews. Martin, this is Janice Hoskins, this summer's one and only sculpture student."

Martin bent his head and shoulders in a rigid, jerky bow. Janice smiled. "Why, how nice to see you here, Dr. Andrews. We've met before, though I'm sure you don't remember."

"We have? I'm terribly sorry, I—"

"Don't be. It was at the spring meetings in New York, and there were so many other people, you couldn't possibly be expected to remember everyone you met."

"Why, Martin," Miranda said, "you're famous."

"Don't be ridiculous, Mandy. I'm not at all."

"Why is it ridiculous? Here we are in the middle of the backwoods, and someone knows who you are."

"Furthermore," Janice said, "I'm not even a microbiologist."

"Then why were you at the meetings?"

"I'm an editor, and I was there looking for books. Your paper was so brilliant I'm sure everybody who publishes in your field must already be after you to write a text."

"Oh, yes, yes, I did get a number of—" His already soft voice trailed off, and he held his hands up, long fingers straight, palms out, as though he were pushing something away from him. At the same time he backed off a few steps and almost stumbled over Miranda. She'd dragged a garden hose over to her bucket of clay and had begun to run water into it, crouching over the pail with the hose in one hand, turning the clods of crumbly earth over with the other to wet them all, and talking softly to herself. "It's pretty dusty, I'll have to let it soak for a day or so before I mix it up, then I'll screen it and see what's left. I suppose I should send some of it to be analyzed, but those men at the state office take forever."

Martin jumped out of her way, and bent down to wipe a few drops of water off his carefully polished cordovans.

"Is Horace here?"

"Yes." She smiled. "He's going to be staying up here full-time this summer."

"How come? What about his agency?"

"He'll run it from here. Most of his business is done on the phone anyway. He's got someone part-time to cover the office and forward the mail and refer the calls up here. If there's anything he has to be in the city for, he can go back for a few days and take care of it."

"That's nice for you. Who else is here? I saw a very thin lady on the road. She had two huge dogs with her."

"Oh, that was Cathleen. She's here to lecture on theater and stagecraft. There, I guess that's enough." She screwed the hose nozzle closed and rose effortlessly, noticed that the hem of her denim skirt was sopping wet, and made a disastrous attempt to wring it dry with her muddy hands. "She's an old friend of Horace's, one of his first clients, as a matter of fact."

"Where's this famous new wheel I'm supposed to inspect?"

She pointed. "The switch is on the side. It's a great gadget, but you have to get used to it."

Martin walked over to a worksink set under the square small-paned window. The aluminum head of the wheel shone against a thick sediment of dried red clay on the bottom of the sink, and the metal drum under the open drain was almost filled with water and slip. "You've already done a lot of work on it, I see."

"I've been up for a while, getting things ready, just like every spring."

9

Martin switched the wheel on, first to slow, then fast. He watched its silvery rotation as though in a trance until Miranda said, "Martin, you're wasting electricity." He jumped a little. "Sorry." He switched the wheel off but kept gazing at it, his lips half-parted, his long solemn face absorbed, his head held a little to one side. Only after it had come to a dead stop did he turn away, almost, Janice thought, as though he were coming to the surface from deep under water. He sighed, rubbed his hand across his eyes, and asked, "When do you start this year?"

"Officially, next week. Right now we've got two people here, Janice and another girl. And Cathleen, that woman you met on the road."

"And Roger," Janice prompted.

"Roger! Is *he* back? Mandy, are you serious? I can't believe you would hire him again."

Eventually Janice said something to fill the silence, since Miranda was obviously not going to. "We just got here this morning," she started to explain, suddenly defensive about her friendship with Roger, "although we meant—" Her remarks were interrupted by a shout from outside. "Mandy! Mandy! Where the hell are you? Look what I've found!"

"Speak of the devil," Janice said.

"In here." Miranda walked to the doorway. "Oh!"

A tall, handsome, black-bearded man was capering across the grass like a somewhat overweight satyr, tugging a young girl after him by the wrist. "It's a very shy, sly nymph," Roger boomed. "So shy she won't even give me her name. You'll have to tell me who she is, Mandy, because otherwise I may die of love without even knowing for whose sake I perish."

The girl giggled and tossed her head, and Miranda said in a voice like a whip, "I've warned you before, Roger, clownish behavior with young students cannot

10

be tolerated.'' The girl cringed. Roger dropped her arm and stepped forward, all his good humor evaporated in a blaze of anger. "Goddammit, Mandy, how dare you talk to me like that!" Miranda, her own anger clamped tight under iron reasonableness, said with commendable calm, "Arlene, my dear, come here and let me introduce you properly.''

The girl, who was still standing exactly where Roger had left her, obeyed meekly. But she really is *very* young, Janice thought. And what kind of a getup is that for walking in the woods? The girl's black skirt was very long and full. With it she was wearing a long-sleeved, high-necked starched white blouse and black ballet slippers. Over her shoulders she'd draped a fringed triangular black silk shawl, pinned at the front with a tiny, old-fashioned cameo. Her light-brown hair was combed smoothly over the top of her head from a center part, puffed out over her ears, and braided and coiled on the nape of her neck. She had a pale, pretty face innocent of all make up.

"Janice, this is Arlene Horowitz. Dr. Martin Andrews, Miss Horowitz. And Professor Benton, Miss Horowitz.''

"Roger.''

She looked up at him and repeated in a soft toneless voice, "Roger.''

"That's right, Arlene.'' He took her hand. "You're going to be one of my students, aren't you?''

"No, she's not," Miranda answered. "She's a pianist.''

Martin moved abruptly. "I've got to go. Goodbye, Miss Hoskins. Goodbye, Miranda.''

"Oh, for God's sake, Martin, you say goodbye as though you were Sydney Carton stepping into the tumbril. Mandy'll be here, you can see her every day you want for the next four months.''

11

"There are times, Roger," Janice observed, "when you depend an awful lot on other people's good manners."

"He has to," Martin said stiffly. "He has none of his own." Janice smiled, and so did Roger, showing small white teeth between hair-fringed lips.

"What I like most about you, Martin, is that now and then, in a very mouselike way, you do try to fight back. It makes it all worth while, somehow."

"I'll walk you to the car," Miranda said, and strolled off with Martin as if neither man had been anything but perfectly polite.

"Oh Roger," Janice began, "why must you—"

"Oh Roger, oh Roger," he mocked. "Because I want to, that's why. He's such an ass!"

"The people in his field all think he's one of the most promising young men they know."

"Big deal. My ambitions do not lie in the direction of being the champion model airplane flier for my age group."

"God, you can be boring."

"And how come you're so interested in Martin's reputation and future? If you've got any ideas about him, dearie, my advice to you is to forget it, he'd never be worth the time and trouble. I know his type, and at your age you ought to, too."

"Why are you being so unpleasant?"

"If there's one thing I will not stand for it's being bossed, and especially by women. So don't try it."

"I'm not—" Stop it, she told herself, what do you care, let Miranda fight it out with him, she started it. But then she couldn't resist adding, "That's still no reason to scapegoat Martin."

"I don't need a reason to scapegoat him. He's a born victim, and I'm a born bully."

"Made for each other, obviously."

"Of course." He looked around. "Hey, where'd she go? I'll be damned if I'll chase her in and out of the trees again."

"Very wise. At your age you might find it wouldn't be worth the time and trouble. You're not getting any younger, you know."

"I don't have to, as long as my girls do."

"You're the ultimate pig!"

"You'd better believe it, baby." He walked up the hill, and she grinned when she heard his cabin door slam.

"Nonsense," Miranda said. "He doesn't mean anything by it, that's just his way. You won't feel like cooking tonight, so do come and eat supper with us."

"Not if Roger's going to be there."

"Oh, Martin, dear, I wish you wouldn't quarrel, it does make things so difficult, and I have so many other worries. Won't you at least try to get along with him?"

"I'm willing to try. It's him. He's the one who always starts it."

"If I promised to talk to him about it, would you come to dinner then?"

"But I—"

"Please? For my sake?"

"Oh, all right. Thanks."

"Wonderful! See you about seven, then."

"Okay." He opened the door of the car, and she put her hand—dirtier than he would have wished—over his and looked up at him, her almond-shaped hazel eyes solemn. "It's so good to have you here. Such a comfort, isn't it, seeing old friends again."

"Well, of course. I always look forward to seeing you again. I don't know why, but I do feel better up here, and the last few weeks especially I've been really looking forward to coming up."

13

"Have you been ill? You do look drawn." He shook his head. "Perhaps you've been working too hard." He frowned, then took a deep breath and said, "I'm—I'm—well, maybe I am a little tired and jittery. But that's all, that's all it is."

"Is something worrying you?"

"No, no."

"We'll talk about it, if there is. A couple of weeks up here and you'll be more relaxed, anyway." He nodded. She patted him into the car and waved as he drove away. Then she walked back to the potting shed. Only Janice was there, absorbed in her sketching.

"Where's Arlene?"

"I don't know. She skittered off up the hill."

"With Roger?"

"No. He's in his cabin. And since there's no other woman around, there's a good chance he's alone."

"Oh." Miranda looked out the door and took a tentative step, then decided against it. Instead, she went over to a shelf of drying pots, took down one that was leather-hard, and fastened it upside down to the wheel with a clay coil. She switched the wheel on low and began to trim the bottom of the pot to make a foot with a modeling tool. Over the wheel's whir she asked, "Have you known him long?"

"Who?"

"Roger."

Oh my, Miranda, Janice thought, that's a big mistake, dear. Aloud she answered. "Long enough."

"Long enough?"

"To have learned what he's like."

"Charming, don't you think?"

"For about twenty minutes at a time, and then as soon as he rolls off you he goes right back to being a sonofabitch."

Miranda said nothing very loudly, and Janice drew a

14

few more pencil lines on her pad. Then she asked, "Why?"

"Why what?"

"Why do you want to know how long I've known Roger?"

"No particular reason, just curious. There, I guess that's enough." She stopped the wheel, stripped off the clay coil, and turned the pot right side up.

"He and Dr. Andrews don't get along very well, do they?"

"Oh, you know how men are," Miranda said. "It's hard to tell whether they really dislike each other, or they're just being what they call competitive."

"My guess, in case you're interested," Janice said, "is that those two really do not like each other. I do know when Roger's role-playing, and when he means it. And as far as Martin is concerned, I'm sure he means it."

2

Martin drove a little further along the top of the mountain until he came to one particular spot on the road where trees had been cleared away on both sides, so that there was an unobstructed view down the slopes of Roundmount, across both valleys, and up the sides of the adjacent blue-green folds in the Berkshire hills. It was part of his ritual for starting each summer at Roundmount for him to stop the car there, get out, and spend a few minutes walking from one side of the road to the other to make sure everything was still the way he remembered it. The complete serenity with which the landscape asserted itself never failed to reassure him, and even this time he could feel himself grow calmer in response to the undemanding quiet beauty around him. He drove the rest of the way to his house in a far more cheerful frame of mind than he would have thought possible when he'd left New York a few hours before, and considerably more grateful at feeling cheerful than he could let himself admit.

His house was set off the road, surrounded on three sides by evergreen trees and underbrush. The porch side faced out over open hay fields bounded by strips of forest, looking like tan sections of a patchwork quilt banded with dark-green featherstitching. An abandoned apple orchard at the end of his land marked the edge of the mountain's steep pitch toward the valley. Martin shivered in the cabin's dank, musty air, and at once went to the fieldstone fireplace that ran across the narrow end of the living room, took hold of the damper, and rattled it open and shut a couple of times. "Move over," he said aloud, "I'm back." A small brown snake, disturbed by the noise, flicked out between the chimneystones above him, slipped down the side of the fireplace, and disappeared into a hole between the hearth and the flat fieldstones of the floor. Martin rattled the damper a few more times as fair warning, then lit the kindling he'd laid as the last act of the previous summer. He went out the door at the side of the fireplace and brought back two of the logs he'd stored on the porch under tarps. When he put the wood on top of the kindling, the dry bark caught at once. Satisfied that the fire was going to burn properly, he opened all the windows and then began to unload the car.

By the time he'd put the house in order and unpacked, it was almost dusk. He showered, changed into fresh clothes, put a flashlight in his jacket pocket, and began to walk down the hill, his shadow long on the

16

road beside him, to eat the first dinner of this summer with Miranda.

The Boardmans, as they were accustomed to do, were serving drinks on the lawn. The deck chairs were arranged in a circle around a tree stump they used as a coffee table. Martin recognized Janice, Arlene, the woman he'd passed on the hill, and Roger in the circle. A middle aged man wearing horn-rimmed glasses was there, and as Martin came closer he was able to decide he didn't know him.

As Martin came up to the circle, Horace Boardman pushed his way backward out of the screen door, carrying a drink in one hand and a tray of ice cubes in the other. He spotted Martin and yelled, "Hi! Look who's here," and waved a hearty welcome, unfortunately with the hand that held the tray. Ice water and chunks of cubes sailed out over the others' heads. Miranda said, "Oh, really, Horace!" Horace looked from his empty tray to the cubes in the grass, laughed, and said, "Oh, damn. Did I get anybody wet?"

"That's all right, Horace, old boy," Roger said. "You'll do anything to get attention, won't you?" He picked an ice cube out of Janice's lap, and after holding it up and inspecting it elaborately on all sides as if it were a jewel, he tossed it across to the icebowl on the stump.

"There's another tray in the icebox. I'll get it."

"You're dating yourself, Miranda," the middle aged man said. "It's not an icebox, it's a refrigerator."

"Electricity came late to our family, Ezra," Miranda replied on her way into the house. "And so did running water."

Martin walked over to Horace. "Good to see you again," Horace said. "Let's see. Have you met everyone? This is Doctor Martin Andrews. Cathleen Linton, and Doctor Ezra Agnew." The men shook hands, and

Horace inspected Martin. "I don't know why Mandy said you were looking peaked. You seem okay to me."

"I am okay. I've just been working very hard, and I'm tired, that's all." Martin thought again that he would never understand why Miranda had married Horace. He was too hearty, altogether too loud, and more than somewhat vulgar. One of the very few times that Martin and Roger had been able to agree on anything was when Roger said that if Horace hadn't decided to be a theatrical agent he would have made a terrific used-car salesman. "It's been one of those winters when I've had to work like a demon to get something finished."

"Will you at least be able to take most of the summer off?"

"A lot of it. Mandy told me you're going to be up here all the time."

"Yep. At least I'll give it a try. If it works out, I'll stay. If it doesn't, I'll go back to coming up when I can. Come on, let's get you a drink."

"In a minute."

"Help yourself then when you're ready. It's all there. I'll talk to you later."

Miranda came out of the house with the ice cubes, and put them in the bowl. "I saw you today," a voice said in Martin's ear. He started. It was Cathleen. "You're the man who passed us on the road."

"Oh, yes, that's right."

"It was such glorious weather, Woglinda and Flosshilde and I simply couldn't resist the idea of a nice long hike."

From across the circle Janice asked, "Where's Wellgunde?"

"Oh, very good! You're familiar with *Das Rheingold*! We're among friends. Alas, my third Rhine maiden got run over by a truck."

18

"Sure it wasn't a submarine?" Roger asked.

"I think I will have a drink after all," Martin said. "May I get you another?"

"No thanks, one teeny one's my limit before dinner." Cathleen waggled her half-full glass so that the ice tinkled and glanced archly at him. "Speaking of Wagner," she went on, turning to Horace, "I had a simply splendid idea this afternoon. Why don't we plan to put on an opera this summer, darling? Wouldn't it be fun?"

"Wouldn't what be fun?" Miranda asked.

"To do an opera this summer. Four or five hours of rehearsal a day for two months, and—"

"Nobody who's coming this summer is studying voice," Miranda replied. "At least nobody I talked to. Do you know anyone who is, Horace?"

"Let me see." Horace was lighting a cigarette with a kitchen match, and while he paused to consider the question the match burned almost down to his fingers. "Ouch," he said, and dropped it, still burning, on the ground. A dead pine needle flared up. "Step on that," Miranda said sharply.

"Not to worry, my dear. It's gone out." He fished another match out of his shirt pocket. "Nope," he finally said. "Sorry, Cathleen. Far as I can remember, all the musical students are instrumentalists, and the drama ones don't sing."

"But they should sing! Nothing's more important to a creative artist than being able to sing properly."

"You may think so," Roger said, "but I don't. And neither do my students. All they're interested in is being able to write. Why would they want to caterwaul?"

"Write—what a barren waste of time. I've never understood why anyone would scribble when it's possible to sing. Fill your lungs, I've always said, and you'll fill your soul." She jumped up, inhaled deeply, rose to her tiptoes, and stretched her arms out wide. "Besides," she added, coming down on her heels again, "writing is just a secondary form of creativity. A writer doesn't actually—"

"That's a lot of—"

"All right, Roger," Miranda interrupted. "Dinner's served. Come on, everyone."

It didn't quite work. They all got up obediently, but as they moved toward the house Roger kept the argument going. "Performers're parasites, pure and simple. All they can do is sing or say what's put in their mouths by the writer. He's the only creative person in the whole business."

"Indeed! Those precious words you're so proud of don't mean a thing on paper, my friend. It's only when a performer takes them over that they ever come alive."

"You mean the writer's words make the performers come alive. Why, when actors or singers have to be themselves, they don't even know who they are. Do you know what the show must go on really means? It means you can't keep me off that stage even if I'm dying, because when I'm not on stage, I disappear." Cathleen sniffed. "Every actor I've ever met suffers from the same delusion that just because it's his silly face that's out front for the people to see, he's the one who's done it all."

"Will you pass your plate, Cathleen?" Miranda was dishing out stew from the head of the table.

"Do you write plays?" Arlene asked. "I thought you were a teacher."

"Roger's very versatile, he thinks," Horace remarked.

"So far I haven't had any complaints."

"Are you here to teach, Dr. Agnew?" Martin asked.

"Ezra, please. No, I'm a psychoanalyst, but this summer I'm back to being a student again. I'm going to

20

paint with Dave Haller.''

"I didn't know old happy Haller was coming back this year." Roger looked accusingly at Miranda. "Since when?" He tasted his stew and made a face. "Whatever you cook always needs salt. I wish you'd learn." Miranda silently handed him the shaker. "Why didn't you say something to me about it? When's Haller coming?"

"I don't know yet."

"But—" Ezra caught Miranda's frown and shut up.

"But what?"

Ezra ignored Roger's question. "Are you also a student?" he asked Martin.

"No. I don't have anything to do with Roundmount at all. I own a summer cabin up the road about half a mile."

"The old slave quarters," Roger explained.

"What are you talking about, Roger? Nobody ever owned slaves here."

"Just joking, Mandy."

"By the way, I didn't tell you, Mandy," Martin said. "I got a letter a while back from a real estate man asking me did I want to sell my house and land."

"Which broker?" Horace asked. "Someone from here?"

"No, in New York, but I don't remember the name. I threw the letter away, but about a week later I got a followup phone call from whoever sent it. Said he was very serious about the offer, and how much was I asking?"

"Sounds like somebody wants to develop up here," Ezra said. "But for what?"

"Ski resort," Horace explained. "Mandy's been approached too. We could sell this place tomorrow for a very sweet price."

"Forget it. Not while *my* name is on the deed. You

21

don't sell family property. Ever.''

"Why not? Somebody sold it to your family," Roger said.

"Some Indian maybe," Miranda retorted. "And that was his business. My family's been here ever since the town was laid out. I do not intend to be the one to leave it."

Janice broke yet another awkward silence. "Where do you go to school, Arlene?"

"I don't."

"Not at all?"

"No. Never have. Don't want to, either."

"Arlene," Miranda put in, "is preparing for a concert career. She's a pianist. Very talented too, I may say. She'll be a credit to Roundmount."

"I don't exist to be a credit to your stupid old music camp." Arlene's face flushed, and without looking at anyone she pushed back her chair and walked out of the room. The others looked after her, and then at each other. Horace started to get up.

"Sit down, Horace," Miranda snapped.

"Artistic temperament, Mandy. It's got to be catered to."

"Nonsense. We're all talented here. That's an adolescent temper tantrum, and I see no reason to encourage that sort of behavior at all."

"Then why do you let Roger get away with it?" Cathleen asked.

"Coffee in the parlor," Miranda said, and the others, with some relief, got up and helped clear the table. Except for Roger, who went through the rooms downstairs till he found Arlene sitting on the staircase, her arms around her knees. "Hello there, nymph," he said. "Feeling unsociable?" She looked at him without answering. He walked up to her and took her wrist. "Play for me."

22

"No."

"Yes." He pulled her up and took her into a room off the hall that had a piano, and closed the door. "I don't feel like it," she said.

"Please?"

"Why should I?"

"Because I asked you to, isn't that a good enough reason? Besides, don't you want to show me you're as good as Mandy says you are?"

She stiffened. "Some other time."

"Promise?"

"If you want." She moved away from him.

"Now where are you going? You're always running away from me. Don't you know you shouldn't do that?" And he grabbed her again and pulled her up against him, his forearms around her waist, lowered his head, and kissed her. She finally managed to twist out of his grasp, push the door open and run back to the dining room. Horace saw her face as she came in, grimaced, and immediately headed for the front hall, where he confronted Roger. Without preamble, he said "Keep your hands off that girl, you bastard."

Roger stared at him. "What the hell's got into you all of a sudden? What makes you think you can tell me what to do?"

Horace cut across him. "If I ever catch you making a pass at her, you'll be sorry."

"Why Horace! You're scaring me to death." And whistling loudly, Roger strolled out and let the screen door slam behind him in Horace's face.

3

Miranda frowned at the list of Sunday concerts, and drummed the eraser end of her pencil against the desk. "This ought to do it," she said, and handed the paper across the desk to Roger, who was checking the schedules. He read it over and raised one eyebrow.

"But you've got Arlene playing every single Sunday."

"That's right."

"How come?"

"You haven't heard her. When you do, you'll know why."

"The other music kids'll kick like hell."

"Let them. I'm not running Roundmount for their benefit."

"Is she honestly that good?"

Miranda nodded.

"Who's she studied with?"

"Her mother, so far. She played for Gelman last month, though, and he agreed to come up five or six times during the summer to supervise her work."

Roger whistled. "She *must* be good. Either that, or her family's got a lot of loot."

"Both. Her father's apparently the kind who thinks he can buy anything."

"If he's got enough money, he can. Where's she from?"

"Chicago."

"How'd she get here?"

"Actually through Horace's cousin Clara. She works for the father, and when she found out they were

24

looking for a music camp for Arlene, she managed to recommend Roundmount."

"That the way the world works, all right."

"It's funny. When a relative tries to do you a favor you never take it seriously because most of the time it ends up not working out. But Horace happened to have to be in Chicago anyway the week that Clara called him, so he was able to hear Arlene play. Once he did, he insisted that she come here. He thinks she's going to have a sensational career."

"As his client, of course. That's Horace for you. Always taking care of number one."

"I will not stand for that kind of remark about my husband. Especially not from you."

"Are you implying you like Horace more than you like me? How can you, Mandy, when you know I like you much more than I do Horace."

"That's an extremely tasteless remark."

"Tastelessness is what I'm famous for."

"If you're so fond of me, Roger, then prove it. Keep away from Arlene."

"What is this? I haven't gone near her."

"The last thing she needs is to have an unhappy love affair with you."

"How do you know? A little unhappy love might make her play all the better."

"Arlene's not as well adjusted as she could be. There's some history of emotional problems, apparently. She certainly does seem to be very young for her age."

"I don't know what the hell that means. For one thing, I don't know anybody who doesn't have emotional problems."

"Don't be difficult. You know that's not the point. The main reason I'm concerned about her being happy here is that I want to make a good impression on

Gelman when he comes up. I want to show him that Roundmount provides the right environment for someone as talented as Arlene. That she gets along well here, and is able to practice and work hard. If I can do that, then he might be willing to teach here next summer."

"And bring his pupils with him."

"Of course. So give me a break, Roger. Don't screw up the best chance I've ever had to turn Roundmount into a big success."

The weather was much too beautiful to sit indoors. Roger was busy helping Miranda, and Janice didn't feel like working anyway, so she went exploring. Walking away from the main buildings, she came across a burnt-out foundation, and poked around in the weed-covered hole for a few minutes on the off chance she might find some artifact she could incorporate as part of a sculpture. Then she walked around what was left of the building trying to visualize what it had once been. It was a house, she decided, not a barn. A big flat stone next to the foundation had obviously been a doorstep. A lilac bush, some bleeding hearts, and a few rosebushes grew wild near it, the remains of what must once have been a garden. She picked one of the roses, wondering what the woman had been like who had planted its ancestor near her back door. The summer's flower, she thought, *this* summer's flower, like everything else has roots that are buried in the past. Here and now always depends on there and then. "Enough of that," she said out loud, "I've gone down that road before and I don't like where it comes out."

Something caught the corner of her eye, and she turned around to face an inquisitive woodchuck. She took a step toward it, and it immediately rumbled away. She noticed it was traveling a path that crossed the field, and with nothing better to do she decided she might just as well see where it went.

It didn't seem to go anywhere in particular on the less forested part of the slope. As soon as it got into the woods proper, though, it took her straight ahead with no more roundabout nonsense, and she walked along easily under the trees, enjoying the dim, cool dampness, her footsteps almost noiseless on the dried pine needles and dead leaves that carpeted the path. The slope was so gradual at first that she was scarcely aware of it; all at once, however, the mountain asserted itself. The trail got very steep and fell off in front of her in three miniature rock bluffs, scarred by bare, almost perpendicular gullies. She hesitated, debating whether she dared make the effort or not. She decided, finally, that if she climbed down backward and hung on to the underbrush and exposed tree roots on either side of the gullies, she'd be able to negotiate them safely, and indeed, she did manage without any real trouble, although she ended a rather undignified scramble down the third and steepest gully ankle deep in a tiny avalanche of pebbles.

Feeling rather pleased with herself, she trekked onward another fifty feet into the forest. Behind her then she heard a familiar sound which she realized was the same rattle of falling stones that had accompanied her slide down that last little precipice. She yelled, "Who's there?" but got no answer. Concluding that she must have loosened some stones that had slipped by themselves, she shrugged and pressed on.

The unexpected noise made her jumpy, though, and she gradually grew certain that behind her someone was making the same muffled, padding noises punctuated by the occasional crackle of dead oak leaves. She stopped and called again, but again got no response. She had a New Yorker's automatic apprehension of any unfamiliar neighborhood, and her awareness, trained by years of city living, clicked over from standby to full alert. The woods were dark and she was alone. The absorbent stifling hush that surrounded her seemed to

27

have deadened every noise except the thudding of her own heartbeat, which was scarcely a reassuring sound considering its speed. No matter how she berated herself for being cowardly and hysterical, she couldn't bring herself to go back up the trail to prove no one was lurking there. On the other hand, she argued silently, she couldn't stand still all day, could she? and so, swearing that she would enroll in a Kung Fu course the day she got home, she forced herself to go forward. Picking up a stout piece of pine branch made her feel a little safer, but any small gain in security was more than wiped out when a jay screamed and flashed across the path in front of her like a blue rocket. After that she scrambled down the hill as fast as she could run until she came to a place on the trail where the path widened into a small but relatively sunny clearing.

The floor of the glade sloped gently to her left, and she followed its slant until she had open ground all around her. At that point, she heard water running, looked down, and saw she was standing not too far from the bank of a brook. It wasn't much of a stream. The water, only a few feet deep, flowed smoothly and almost silently on a warty bed of solid stone, slipping over the rounded pebbles that lined its course, eddying around larger rocks and great glacial monoliths still resisting the persistent gentle washing. Janice waited, tense and alert. Time passed. Nothing happened, nobody came, no one attacked, the brook continued its leisurely trickle, and her panic ebbed away with its flow until she was finally calm enough to decide she was being silly, that no one was actually after her. She stayed where she was, though, unwilling to leave the sunlight, her eye caught by the way the water changed color when it passed from light to shade: clear white in the sun, dull brackish-brown in the shadows of the over-hanging branches. She'd almost forgotten how frightened she'd been when a twig crackled behind her and she whirled, clutching her stick for dear life and terrified all over again.

Horace Boardman was heading straight for her across the clearing. Janice relaxed. She'd known Horace for almost a week, and she knew he was no threat to her. He was peering at his watch, apparently having trouble reading it in the gloom because he stopped to hold his wrist in a ray of light. She said, "Horace! Why didn't you answer me when I yelled?" To her delight, he jumped almost as much as she had at the bluejay's screech.

"Where the hell did you come from?"

"From up the hill. Like you."

"Me?" He pointed his thumb back over his shoulder. "I came in from the road." She looked past him and saw another faint track at right angles to the path down which she'd just fled. "But weren't you following me?"

"Following you?" He peered around the clearing. "What makes you think you were followed? Did you see anybody?"

"No, but I heard him."

He stared at her. "You're sure it was a him?" His drawl conveyed such wariness of the kind of women whose sexual fantasies lead them to accuse innocent and virtuous men, that Janice couldn't help flushing. "You must've been imagining things," he went on. "These woods can get spooky if you're not used to them."

"I wasn't imagining!"

He moved, ever so casually, further away from her. Why the bastard, she thought, half furious, half amused. He wants me to know he thinks he's got to be careful. He solemnly inspected the brook. "Guess there won't be much swimming this summer by the looks of it."

"It's pretty shallow water to swim in."

"Lower than usual this year. We had a kinda dry spring." He looked around the clearing again. "It's deeper around the bend." He walked off, then turned and said, "Aren't you coming? I'll show you." She followed, making sure she kept a fair distance away from him. The brook curved sharply, split in two against an enormous boulder, then slid together on the other side into a dark brown whirlpool about ten feet across. "Pothole," he said, pointing. "It's plenty deep enough, but I don't advise swimming in it, not unless you like leeches."

"Leeches! Ugh!"

"It's all right back there, and you can always swim in that shallow part when it's clear and clean. But don't try to swim there when it's muddy, like after a rain, and whatever you do, don't go into this pothole, ever. It's very dangerous. Not because of the leeches. It's full of snapping turtles, and it'd be one helluva hole to dive into, I'll tell you that."

"Don't worry, you won't catch me near it."

"Just wanted to warn you." He grinned. "Can I give you a lift up the hill, or do you want to commune with nature some more? It's easy walking down, but it's a long climb from here."

"Are you leaving? You just got here."

"That's all right. I only came to check out how deep the water is. Somebody's sure to want to go swimming the minute it gets warmer."

He led her out to his car, pulled way off the road out of sight. On the way up, they passed Cathleen and her two dogs heading down hill. She waved and Horace waved back. Oh ho, Janice thought. So much for checking out the old swimming hole. Horace dropped her in front of the main house, turned quickly around in the driveway, and went back downhill. I wonder if Miranda knows, Janice thought, and if she doesn't, I'm not about to be the one who tells her.

4

Martin had tackled his personal problem in the same strictly rational, unemotional way he analyzed every other intellectual issue, and as he saw the situation, to get back to his old self again, logically he had to do two things: rest up enough to restore his energy, and re-establish a decent work schedule. It's true, nobody at the institute knew or cared when or how he showed up at the lab; nonetheless, for his own sake, it was obvious he had to conquer his paralysis and start working again. No more reading detective stories until four or five in the morning and then dozing till noon so that he wasn't sleepy and stayed up all the next night reading again. No more evenings in the local bar. No more wasting time with trips to museums and zoos. No more afternoons in the movies. In a way he sort of regretted giving up the feeling of freedom, but he couldn't spend the rest of his life loafing; he wasn't built that way.

When he'd first noticed that he wasn't able to get anything *done* anymore, he hadn't cared. He'd just finished slaving to get his paper finished in time for the meetings, and at that point he was so tired that nothing mattered. The brilliance of his work, as he'd expected it would, had helped to clinch his appointment as a permanent fellow of the institute (and the youngest man ever named, at that), an honor no one could overestimate. Just the same, only since he'd reached this goal had Martin begun to realize how much it had taken out of him, and he sometimes wondered, while he lay fretfully sleepless, whether any fellowship—even this one—was actually worth that vast an expenditure of energy. What good was being successful if it meant you had to put so

31

much into achieving it that you didn't have anything left over to go on with?

After three totally lazy and unproductive months, however, the excuse of past effort began to sound somewhat lame. It was time, Martin told himself, to snap out of it and get going again, and Roundmount was without question the best place to start. His plan was simple enough. The thing to do first was tire himself out so he'd have to go to bed. Once he'd got back in the habit of sleeping during the night like everybody else, he'd get some real rest and be able to work easily again, the way he always had. The day after he arrived, therefore, he conscientiously did as much hard labor around the cabin as he could find to do, and took three long walks. The exercise did help. By the end of the day he was physically so worn out that he was glad to go to bed early, fell asleep instantly, slept right through till seven, and woke optimistic and refreshed. The second day he followed the same regime and again fell asleep without trouble; but then, to his dismay, after four hours he woke up for good, which certainly didn't seem much of an improvement. He lay in bed till six, then got up feeling as though he hadn't slept at all. Despite his depression and fatigue, though, he chopped a lot of wood, then tramped stubbornly up and down the mountain trails till dusk. He staggered to bed at ten, and again fell asleep with no trouble, but once more was wide awake long before dawn.

Savagely determined to beat this ridiculous weakness once and for all, he forced himself to get up in the chilly blackness, lit a fire, took a cold shower, and made and ate breakfast. Then, disregarding a curiously ominous reluctance, he marched himself over to the desk, sat down, opened his briefcase, and picked up some papers. No sooner had he begun to read the top sheet than he was doubled over by a sudden jolt of intense pain that stabbed through his midsection like a knife, washed out over his whole body, and ebbed back into his abdomen. He ran for the john, certain he was going to vomit. He didn't, though it took every bit of control he could muster not to. Shaken and sore, he stumbled back to bed as soon as the pain subsided, and lay there apprehensively waiting for his indigestion to recur. When, by nine, it hadn't, he got up, took another shower (he needed it—he was as sweaty and feeble as if he'd played two sets of tennis), dressed, locked the papers up in the desk against the field mice, and left the house.

He wandered around his own property for a while, then started to cross lots aimlessly, coming out of the trees into the upper pasture. As he trudged across the field, his eyes on the early summer grass in front of him, he heard his name called the way it always was in his worst nightmares, in a thin, soft, clear wail:

"M-a-a-r-t-i-i-n!"

He spun on his heel, his heart pounding, his body prickly with waves of terror. There was nobody there. The distant summons was repeated: "M-a-a-r-t-i-i-n!" This second shock coming almost on top of his earlier attack was too much for him. "I'm going crazy!" he thought, scanning wildly a landscape he already knew, with sickening conviction, was completely deserted.

Then he heard a giggle, and an entirely human and conversational voice said, "Look up here, you silly."

He lifted his head and saw Arlene Horowitz's laughing face peering down from a ledge that was the half-buried end of a buff-colored boulder. "Come up and talk to me."

"Talk to you? What the hell do you think you're doing up there?"

"Oh, please—don't be mad." She smiled. "Only for a minute, I have to get back to the cabin and practice." He took one reluctant step forward. "Go around there,

33

it's easier," she said, and pointed to the left. He climbed the hill, skirting the ledge and a few bushes, and came out in back of her.

"Were you so scared because you thought I was a ghost?"

"Don't be silly," he replied brusquely. "What makes you think I was scared?"

"The way you jumped when I called your name, that's all." She giggled again. "It's easy to scare people. Sometimes you don't even have to say anything, just sort of hang around or follow them through the woods. Why don't you sit down?"

He eased himself onto the flat, lichen-covered rock. "What're you doing out here, anyway?"

"This." She bent her head forward and flipped her hair, which was hanging loose down her back to her waist, over her head, so that her face was buried. "I washed my hair," her voice came muffled from underneath, "and I'm drying it in the sun."

"It certainly is long."

"Uh huh." She began to brush it in vigorous strokes away from the scalp out to the ends, which floated and snapped and sparkled in the light.

"Do you have to go through all this every time you wash it?"

"Uh huh." With another quick movement she threw her head up and back, so that her hair flew out. Facing him, she began to brush it down, smoothing it out.

"How many years did it take to grow that long?"

"Most of my life. I trim the ends off even myself when they need it, but I never have it cut." She paused to tug at a snarl. "When I was a little girl my mother made me cut some of it off for the summers, but since I've been old enough to do what *I* want, I've just let it grow and grow."

"But it must be a lot of trouble to take care of."

"It's not trouble, I love doing it." She put the brush down, bent her head slightly, and with skillful fingers divided the hair into three hanks and began to plait these tightly into a single thick braid. "I've done this so many times," she said as she worked, "that I once had the idea that if I could only talk to it the right way, my hair would braid itself. You'd think it could—it's had enough practice." She gave a soft laugh. "It wouldn't though, no matter how I coaxed it." But as Martin stared, his eyes squinted against the sunlight, at the movements of her flickering weaving hands, it looked as though the glossy strands were spinning themselves into a brown ribbon, settling where they belonged the way the feathers on a folding bird's-wing come to rest properly after stretching themselves out flat, then wriggling into the right order.

"Oh, darn—"

"What's the matter?"

"My elastic broke. Here, hold the end, will you, so it won't come undone?" She held the braid out to him, and without thinking, should I shouldn't I, he automatically took it. "I've got another one in my pocket." She began to rummage around in the lap of her black skirt.

The lustrous plait lay across his palm like a live thing, damp, soft, thick, heavy. He moved his fingers on it slightly, and felt the individual hairs slip over one another, grating against themselves with an almost inaudible rasp. He closed his hand. The hair was so thick that even at the end his fingers barely reached around. Suddenly and overwhelmingly he wanted to yank hard on this silky rope, to pull it back and down with all his strength. Unaware of what he was doing, he slid his hand up toward her skull and the root of the braid, and his grip tightened. A picture came into his mind of how she'd look as he held her captive like that—her face up to the sky and the front of her slim throat exposed. In the picture her mouth was open and she was screaming.

"Ouch! Be careful! You're pulling."

"Sorry." He dropped the hair rope, and wiped the palms of his hands on his chinos.

"I've got it." Catching up the braid with her left hand, she snapped an elastic band around its end, twisting the rubber until it was tight enough to hold the hairs in place.

"Too bad I didn't have an inkwell handy," he said, hideously certain that somehow she knew what had gone through his mind. She didn't reply. Unable to bear the silence, he cleared his throat and went on, "Tell me, how do you like Roundmount?"

She paid no attention to this overture, either, except to glance up at him. Running her hands across her thighs, she said, "What did I do with—oh, here." She brought two tortoise shell combs out of her lap, and carefully slid them into her hair over her ears. "I can't bear to have it pull too tight on top," she explained. "Maybe other girls can, but I can't. I guess my scalp is more sensitive. And I have to pin it back with these combs, otherwise it's so heavy it drags. These're the only combs I've ever been able to find that're exactly right. It has to be just so, or I can't stand it." Finally satisfied with their placement, she pulled her braid over her left shoulder, stroked it lovingly into position along the hollow of her neck, and patted the end, which dangled between her small breasts, approvingly. "There, that's better." She focused on him. "Did you say something before?"

"Just asked how you like Roundmount."

"It's all right. I like the horseback riding a lot." Very daintily, using only her thumb and forefinger, she began to pluck loose hairs out of her brush. "What do you think of it?"

"It's a good school. Miranda does a fine job."

"You're very fond of her, aren't you?"

"Who, Miranda? Sure, we've—we're old friends."

"Does she like you as much as you like her?"

"Why, what an extraor—I guess so, I certainly hope so."

She used her soft laugh again. "I'm sure she must." She finished cleaning out her brush, and began to wind the cloudy nest of single hairs together into a neat little coil. "By any chance did she ever tell you why she was so anxious to get me here as a student?" He shook his head. "There must be some reason. I'll bet it's because she hopes Daddy'll endow the camp. I'll bet that's why."

"I don't understand. Miranda doesn't—"

"He's very rich." She peered at him. "Don't you believe me?"

"But I—"

"Come on, I'll show you his picture." She gathered her brush and comb and pile of hairs, pushed them all into her skirt pocket, and stood up. "Come on."

He got up unwillingly. "Where?"

"Up to my practice cabin, it's over there." She pointed to the right, and began to move.

"But there's no cabin in this field."

She stopped dead. "Yes, there is, up there." She pointed again.

"It wasn't here last year, then."

"Are you sure of that?" She stared at him, alarmed and intent.

"Of course I'm sure," he replied testily. "I know what's on every square yard of this place."

"Absolutely sure?" she pleaded.

"Yes, yes. Why won't you believe me?"

"I believe you." She fingered her braid, rubbed the end against her cheek, put it in her mouth, and gnawed on the hairs. Then she dropped it and straightened her shoulders. "Come on, I'll show you anyway."

They walked up the hill without speaking. The minute Martin saw the cabin he was positive all over again that it was new. It wasn't anything like the other practice cabins: tiny soundproofed clapboard shacks, just large enough to shelter a practicing musician and give him some privacy and the rest of the camp some peace. This was much bigger—a one-room house almost as big as his own, sheathed with yellow-new, unweathered split shingles.

"The door's over here." She led him around the corner, and Martin said, "Pretty fancy, I must say— none of the other cabins have picture windows."

"No? That doesn't surprise me." She pushed the door open, walked in, turned around, actually curtseyed, and said, primly, "Won't you come in?" as though she were welcoming him to a child's make-believe tea party. He stepped in past her, and she followed him into the room, leaving the door a little ajar behind her. She switched on a light—despite the windows the room seemed dark after the glare of the meadows—and he looked around curiously. The cabin had a minimum of social furniture: two armchairs flanking a fieldstone fireplace, a couple of tables and lamps. Most of the floor space was taken up by an opened Steinway concert grand that loomed hugely black in the middle of the room. The piano rack was covered with music, and more music lay on the floor under the piano and around the room in untidy heaps. An elaborate tape deck and cassette machine, surrounded by boxes of tape, stood on a table across from the piano where it would catch every bit of sound.

"Do sit down." Arlene gestured toward one of the chairs.

"Thank you." Martin bowed, strangely unable to

keep from falling in with her stilted, unreal conversation. "I regret to say I can only stay a minute."

"Oh, dear, that is too bad." She draped one hand and arm along the edge of the piano as though she were posing for a portrait; Martin, still standing, picked up a silver-framed photograph from the table. "Are these your parents?"

"Yes." She came over and sat down, and so did he. "That was taken right after they were married."

"You look very much like your mother."

"She's a lot darker than I am. She was a pianist, you know, but she gave up her promising career when she married Daddy and had me and my brother, Bernard. He lives at home with them all by himself now. Too bad for him, but," her tone expressed both regret and satisfaction, "it can't be helped, can it?"

Martin couldn't think of anything to say, and Arlene went on, after a few minutes, "She could've been a great artist."

"Who, your mother?"

"Yes."

"Did she play professionally?"

"Oh, yes. She met Daddy during her first concert tour, and he fell in love with her right away and pursued her all over the country until he got her to say yes. Don't you think that's romantic?"

"Oh, yes."

"Once they got married, although they were very poor, of course he made her stop playing and stay at home, the way a wife was expected to do."

"Is that what you're going to do, give concerts like your mother?"

"I guess so. I suppose I have to, don't I? Otherwise, what good is all this—?" and she looked around the room.

"Don't you want to?"

"No! I hate playing in public, hate it!"

"Then why?"

"Well, don't you see, I can't help it? I've studied for so many years, and it's cost so much money, and my mother's spent her time giving me lessons instead of having her own career and being a famous artist, and I've had every advantage. They'd all be wasted if I wasn't grateful, if I didn't use them, wouldn't they? My parents expect it of me, and they've made so many sacrifices so I could. And besides," she added, her voice proud, "I'm talented. I must live up to that responsibility."

"But if you don't want to—"

She stood up. "I must practice now. Miranda's already scheduled me to play, and it's been so long since I've performed for a real audience, not just other—" Her hand went up to her braid and she began to finger its end.

Martin replaced the photograph and started for the door.

"Wait," she said. "I've got something to tell you."

"What?"

"I'm sorry I was so mean before, truly I am, especially now when I see you're really nice."

"I don't understand."

"Yes you do. When I scared you from the rock like that. I knew it would, that's why I did it. I like to scare people a lot. But this time, honest, I'm sorry."

"How did you know that calling my name would scare me?"

She said, very simply, "Because we have the same bad dreams."

He stared at her stupefied, then turned away. "I must go, you've got to practice." As he put his hand on the knob, someone knocked on the door from the outside and a man's voice said, "Anybody home?" The door

40

was pushed open all the way. Martin stepped to one side to avoid being hit. Roger was on the doorstep.

"Hello nymph."

"Hello." Arlene stood in front of the door, blocking his entrance. Martin stepped out to stand at her side.

"Well, if it isn't young Dr. Andrews surprised in *flagrante delicto*! Now that's what I call quick work, Martin. Why, you only met her a couple of days ago, and here you both are, set up in a tidy little love nest. And I'll bet that Mama Miranda doesn't know a thing about it."

"Benton, you're unspeakable!" He bowed to Arlene. "Good morning." As he passed her, he touched the outside doorknob and looked at her. She nodded almost imperceptibly. He pushed his way out past Roger, holding on to the knob so that the door closed tight behind him. They heard a click as the latch snapped into place, and another click as Arlene turned a key.

"Goddammit!"

Martin allowed himself one small smile, and walked away. Roger began to pound on the door. "Hey Arlene, open up, I want to talk to you!"

Inside Arlene began to practice octave scales *fortissimo e prestissimo*; their dazzling rise and fall followed Martin till he was out of earshot. As for Roger, he stood on the doorstep listening for a while, then grinned, tipped an imaginary hat, and walked off saying to himself, Oh my yes. For once Horace is right. That will be quite a career.

5

"What's the trouble between you two?" Ezra asked. "That night at dinner it was obvious he didn't know you

41

were coming because Miranda hadn't wanted to tell him."

"I'll bet he wasn't too pleased to find out, either." Dave Haller came around the easel and squinted at Ezra's painting.

"No, he wasn't." Ezra leaned back to let Dave see.

"After last summer I'm not sure I should've come back, anyway." Dave pointed. "That's a lot of texture there in that corner. I focus on the surface too much when I look at it."

Ezra considered, his head on one side. "It's not finished yet. I have something in mind."

"Okay." Dave shrugged amiably and went back to his own canvas.

"What happened last summer?"

"Tell you later. Let's work, the light's too good to waste."

After a half-hour, Ezra said, "Coffee?" Dave nodded, and Ezra went over to a counter where a kettle of water was steaming over a hot plate, dumped unmeasured instant coffee into two none too clean plastic cups, filled the cups with water, and stirred the liquid with the handle of a brush. Dave got up and stretched. "Time for a break," he said, and walked over to the open door of the art shed. Ezra brought the coffee and stood by him, leaning against the door jamb.

"It sure is lovely."

"Yeah. It's always been great here. But this summer, for some reason, the atmosphere's gone wrong. Maybe it's Horace. I don't understand why he suddenly decided to hang around."

"Doesn't he always come up here in the summer? I thought the place belonged to the two of them, that they both ran it."

"No. Horace has his own business. He's a theatrical agent with his own office. Usually he sniffs around up

42

here each summer to see if there's anyone talented enough for him to be interested in. He's even signed a couple of the acting kids. But most of the time he stays in town and comes up weekends. That is, he used to."

"Maybe business is lousy, and he's filling his time by working up here."

"That's possible. Roundmount's Mandy's baby. She inherited this old farm and got the idea of turning it into a crafts camp, set it up, and nursed it through the tough years by herself. Horace's never had anything much to do with it before." Dave sipped his coffee and made a wry face. "Boy, these cups really need washing. The thing is, Mandy's an artist herself, a wonderful potter, so she understands what creative people are all about from the inside. Horace doesn't. He doesn't have the right vibes. When he talks about the theater, for instance, he doesn't mention writing or acting or directing or scene designing. He talks about contracts and deals and properties, and how he was able to sell the movie rights for more money than anybody else ever could."

"The biz end of show biz? That's where the real power is."

"Yeah, but that kind of power isn't what Roundmount's about. Not that Mandy's weak. She knows what she wants and God help you if you get in her way. But a place like this can only work when the people who come here feel cherished and appreciated. Atmosphere's a part of that. It's nebulous, but it's real. Horace doesn't know about cherishing for art's sake, just for money's sake. This place is just a piece of property to him, like his clients are. He'd sell it in a minute if he could get enough money for it. Mandy never would. She'll struggle till she dies if she has to. She might close up, but she'd never sell out."

"Interesting. But not our problem."

"No. Back to work."

"Okay." After a little while Ezra put his brush down and stepped back to inspect what he'd done. "Dammit to hell," he said. "You were right."

"What about?"

"That texture. It is too much."

"Let's see." Dave came over. "Uh huh. I think if you smooth it off a little over here—"

"Yes, that might do it." Ezra took a palette knife and began to scrape at the paint surface. As he worked he said, "You know, to get back to the beginning of this conversation, you still haven't told me what the trouble is between you and Roger."

"Oh, it's a long story." Dave peered around Ezra's arm. "Hey, not too much, you don't have to take it all off."

"I'm not going to take it all off. Don't be such a mother hen. What did Roger do to you?"

"He never did anything to me, what gave you that idea?"

"Who, then?"

"Oh, all right, if you must know. It was one of his students, nobody special but a nice enough girl. She had a thing going with him at the beginning of the summer, so everything was fine, but then she got interested in another student and after that Roger did his best to make her life miserable. I guess the idea that she got tired of him before he was ready to drop her was more than he could take. Anyway, one day I got fed up listening to him complain about how stupid she was, and told him he ought to know better than to let his personal feelings get mixed up in his job. And I meant it too. For crissakes it's hard enough to teach anybody anything under the best of circumstances without dragging a lot of extraneous personal crap into it. And he told me to mind my own business, and then one thing led to another and we ended up having a big fight that went on for the rest of the summer."

Ezra chuckled. "Nothing like a little frankness to cloud the air."

"You said it. Turn it blue was more like it. We both lost our tempers. I heard later that the two kids got married in the fall, and that for a wedding present Roger sent them a couple of dueling pistols tagged His and Hers."

"You're kidding."

"No, it's true, so help me." Dave grinned. "It is kinda funny. But the thing is, someday he's liable to cause real trouble around here."

Ezra nodded. "Oh, yes. That kind of childish person sooner or later usually does."

"Excuse me." Janice put her head in the door of the studio. "Sorry to interrupt, but Miranda asked me to post these schedules, and one of them's marked for the bulletin board in here."

"Right over there. Which schedule is it?"

"Sunday concerts." She held the sheet out to Dave, who scanned it. "That's funny," he said, "I see that girl Arlene is down for every single Sunday afternoon."

"Is that unusual?"

"Sure is. A lot of musical people from New York come up to the Berkshires, and there's always some of them in the audience on Sundays. It's sort of a showcase for the music students, and ordinarily nobody gets to play more than twice a month." He handed the paper back to Janice. "I guess Mandy thinks she's worth showing off."

The feeling he was being watched made Martin look up and out. Arlene was sitting on his porch step, gazing at him through the screen. He was so startled that he half leaped out of his chair.

45

"How long have you been there?"

"A few minutes. It's such a nice day I thought maybe you'd come take a walk with me."

"Now?" She nodded. "Well, I hadn't planned—"

"Don't you ever do anything you hadn't planned?" She got up and peered in at him, and he remembered his manners.

"You could—er—come in and sit down for a minute if you want to."

"Won't you come out? My father says walking is the best exercise there is."

"I'd like to, honestly, but I—I can't."

"Then I'll come in." She opened the door, brushed past him, and composed herself in the corner of his sofa. "Sit down," she invited him, waving a hand at his chair. "Oh, yes—thanks," and he sank back into it.

She bent toward him, and the wicker arm of the sofa creaked under her weight. "I suppose you're wondering what the real reason is I came to see you without being invited or anything?"

"Certainly not—I—you just told me why."

"No," she insisted, "I mean the *real* reason. You know what that is? I've decided I can trust you."

"That's a very nice thing to say, I'm sure, but I don't quite—"

She paid no attention to the feeble interruption.

"You're not part of Roundmount, that's why."

"Arlene, I don't—what are you talking about?" Without understanding it, Martin knew that he wanted to—that he had to—stop this conversation, that he didn't want to hear what she was going to say, but he couldn't even begin to head her off before she was speaking again, becoming less composed with every word.

"Yes you do, you do know why, I'm sure you do, because we're alike, you see. I know it, I can't be wrong

46

about it—"

"Arlene, I—"

"I told you the other day, we have the same bad dreams and you knew what I meant then. And you knew right away I had to be saved from Roger and you did it. So that's why I decided I could come to you, that you would help me." She jumped up from the sofa, ran across the room, knelt on the floor in front of him, and clasped his legs.

"What are you *doing*?" His voice rose to a screech, and he cowered as far away from her as the back of the chair would let him.

"You're my only hope," she said and began to cry. "It's the same for both of us. Everybody either picks on us or they use us, that's all they think we're good for."

"No, no! I don't know what you're talking about, I won't listen to you!" He clapped his hands over his ears.

"Yes you do know! It's true, you've got to say it's true!" Still leaning against his legs, she reached up and tugged at his arm. He twisted his head away to bury it in the chair cushion. Her voice, insistent, rapid, went on, "But if we fight them together, I'm sure we can manage, honest I am, Martin. I can help you, really I can, but you've got to help me, the way you did the other day with Roger. If I could do it by myself I wouldn't ask you, but I can't, I'm not strong enough, they took me back too soon."

"I can't help you! Leave me alone! I don't even know what you're talking about! Leave me alone, will you?" He wriggled free of her grip and sprang up, shoving her out of his way with such force that she fell over on the floor. He escaped to the door and stood with his back to it, panting, watching her, ready to run out if he had to. She started to get up, looked at his face and sank back, put her cheek down on her bent knees, and wrapped her

47

arms around her legs. "Oh God," she sobbed, rocking a little, "all those people, all those concerts—I can't possibly do it, I know I can't. Please, isn't there anybody here to help? I need help, God. Why do you let them all use me? Send somebody to help me, please, please!"

Still poised for flight, Martin stared at her, unwilling to believe this was happening, fighting for self-control. He was finally able to say, "Arlene, get up, get up, stop that silly crying. It's—it's—undignified. Supposing someone should hear you? What would they think?"

"Undignified?" Without raising her head from her knees she laughed and sobbed together. "If that's all you think you've got to worry about, you're wrong. You're the one that's silly, because you need help as much as I do."

"That's not true, I'm fine, I'm fine! There's nothing the matter, nothing." He drew a deep, ragged breath. He came toward her cautiously and tendered his hand. "Come on, get up like a good girl."

She rocked back and forth a few more times, still sobbing, then stopped abruptly and shook her head. "You can't help me," she said, and wiped the tears off her face with her knuckles. "I'll have to think of something else." Disdaining his hand, she rose in one fluid movement, completely self-possessed, all emotion erased from her face.

"Goodbye." She walked past him and out the door, closing the screen quietly behind her. Martin didn't turn around to watch her go. Instead he looked down at his still outstretched hand, then clenched it into a fist and covered it with his other hand, cradling it against his body as if he'd been hurt. "Why," he said aloud, listening to his own voice as if it were somebody else speaking, "Why—that's such a terrible thing, isn't it? But what could I do? I mean, really—it's terrible."

48

6

The instant the last student had registered, Miranda put up a notice announcing the picnic supper, Round-mount's only official social event. The reason she held it so promptly was that she could still be fairly certain that almost everyone would be talking to everyone else. Summer feuds, to Miranda, were simply a fact of life, and she knew that if she ran her party even a week later it would look less like a social event than a truce meeting for the members of many small armed camps. She also used the picnic to pay her social debts to people in Lees-field.

She arrived at the festivities with the guest lecturer for the week, a professor of art history, and his wife in tow. Roger was already playing his favorite game of harem, lying in the grass, his hands behind his head, expounding to a group of adoring females. Among them, Miranda was distressed to see, was Arlene. Barely able to suppress her anger, she brought the Apfelhugels over to Dave Haller and introduced them. They chatted for a couple of minutes about the manifest glories of the New England countryside; eventually Dave, reliable and true, bent forward with flatteringly exaggerated interest and asked, "What are you planning to talk to us about, Professor Apfelhugel?" and Miranda was able to edge away.

"My topic," she heard the professor say as she was leaving, "is Cupid versus Cupidity: The Role of the God of Love in the Fiduciary Aspects of the Art of the Early Merovingians."

"Indeed? That should be interesting!"

"Ja, I find it so," the professor said complacently,

49

and his wife, a Nordic edition of a Radcliffe intellectual, nodded emphatic agreement. "You see—" Dave took a minute off to consider the matter of Frau Professor Apfelhugel's dress, and concluded that her decision to wear plaid Bermuda shorts was nothing less than disastrous, roughly the equivalent of seeing Flagstead play Brunhilde in a bikini. "As a matter of fact," the professor was saying when he started to listen again, "you Americans a popular song in the nineteen-thirties had, that summarizes up the topic of my lecture perfect."

"Is that so?" Dave said encouragingly, absolutely certain that he hadn't missed anything vital.

"Ja, you know—" he paused for effect, "the line that goes, the rich get rich and the poor get children." His wife smiled proudly, and Dave managed a hollow laugh which, with the instinct of a pedagogue, Apfelhugel immediately recognized as not genuine. Wrinkling his academic brow, he explained his joke to the dull pupil. "Listen, you see, it's like this, the rich get rich is cupidity, and the poor get children is Cu—"

"Roger," Miranda said, "help?"

"Sure thing."

"Is there anything we could do, Miranda?" one of his girls offered languidly.

"Not right now Alison. In a little while you may help serve hamburgers."

"That sounds like great fun." Alison held her hand out to Roger. He pulled her up from the ground with such force that he had to catch and hold her tight against him to keep her from falling forward.

"There he goes again. Honestly!" The maneuver had been observed by the dance teacher, who nudged her friend and constant companion.

"Who, what?"

"Roger the lodger, with that pretty little blonde."

"She is pretty, isn't she?" The friend and companion appraised Alison's looks with an expert's eye, then sighed and shook her head regretfully. "You might as well relax about Roger," she advised. "He'll never change."

"I guess you're right. I don't know what Miranda sees in him, anyway."

"What do you care? You don't have to." The ladies exchanged mutually congratulatory glances.

"Who are those two charmers?" Three of the last students to arrive were clumped together, warily inspecting the thirty or so people who had gotten there first. "Where? Oh, those two. The one in the white blouse teaches dance, and the other viola, I think."

"That's a relief. I won't have to have anything to do with either of them. The one in the sandals and the pointed hat looks like Caligula in drag."

"What does that mean?"

The tall thin boy looked down at his companions. "Where did you say you went to school?"

The girls looked puzzled. "Ohio," they answered, in chorus. "Why?"

"Nothing, cupcakes. Forget the whole thing."

"Anything I can do, Miranda?"

"Oh, Martin, yes there is. Go talk to somebody, if you don't mind, this one's not going too well. Nobody seems to be mixing."

Martin walked over toward Janice, who was standing with a short, sandy-haired young man. As he went by Arlene, she nodded to him as though the scene at his house that afternoon had never happened.

". . . and they used a *cremorne*, can you imagine?" the boy was saying passionately to Janice. "A

51

cremorne! A noble instrument, devised solely to play sad music, invented to be used only at *funerals*—and here they were, playing jazz with it in a *night* club!"

"Well, that's show biz," Janice said. She smiled at Martin. "Hi," she said gratefully. "This is Robert Deland, Dr. Martin Andrews."

They shook hands. "Bob here was just telling me," she went on brightly, "of his fascinating hobby. He reproduces old instruments." She took a gulp of her beer and muttered into the glass, "And he's the boy who can do it, all right."

"What kind of instruments?"

"Wind, mostly. I've just finished restoring an oboe da caccia, and now I'm working on a serpent." Deland's pale blue eyes gleamed behind his glasses, and his long nose twitched.

"Oh, yes? What does a serpent sound like?"

"A deep open tone. Rather like a human voice. Though actually," Deland confessed, "I've never heard one played. The ones at the museum are naturally in disgraceful condition."

"Naturally," Janice said. Conversation stopped, and Deland looked around. "If you'll excuse me—"

"By all means." Janice turned to Martin. "Young, isn't he?"

"I guess so." He stared at her blankly, and she thought, well, you're certainly not much help in a social situation, are you? Aloud, she said, "I haven't seen you around since we ate dinner together last week."

"I've been rather busy."

"I'm sure you have." She went on, grimly determined to keep some conversation going, "I understand Arlene is playing tonight."

"Oh, is she?"

"Yes. I'm looking forward to hearing her. What a strange girl she is, though."

"Why do you say that?"

"You don't think it's odd for someone to dress as though she were living in 1875?"

"Does she? I don't know anything about women's styles."

"My guess is she thinks of herself as a reincarnation of Clara Schumann. She does look like her, you know."

"Don't be absurd," Martin said sharply. "Are you implying she's mentally deranged?" And in his mind, unbidden, Arlene's voice repeated, "We're alike. You need help as much as me."

"What a nice way to put it," Janice said, annoyed at being put on the defensive. "If you're asking me, I'd say yes, she is, she's probably as nutty as a fruitcake."

"Are you a doctor?"

"You know I'm not."

Martin clicked his tongue disapprovingly. "An unprofessional opinion on a medical matter, if you don't mind my saying so, can be dangerous. And that particular opinion is certainly not kind."

"I don't pretend to be either kind or professional," Janice retorted. "I think I'll go see if I can help with the food." She sloped off to get another beer first. Horace was tending bar, which meant he was fishing cans of beer out of a washtub filled with ice, opening them, and handing them out.

"Can I have another?"

"Sure thing." He pulled the tab for her and dropped the strip into the tub.

"Who's that tall blonde man talking to Mandy?"

"Name's Owen Henderson. He's police chief in Leesfield. Mandy likes to keep her fences mended."

"A cop?"

"Yep. Want to meet him? You could tell him about being followed through the woods."

"I'm sure he'd be fascinated." She took her beer and

her annoyance and walked away to the fireplace where Roger and two of his entourage were shoveling charred hamburgers into sliced pasty-white hamburger buns. Janice broke one open and shuddered. The patties were still cold in the middle, the red meat studded with hard little islands of unmelted fat.

"Aren't you even going to warm the buns?"

"What for?" One of the girls gave her a mean look.

"Please, Janice," Roger said peevishly. "This is the American way of life you're criticizing. Just put enough ketchup on them and you'll never know the difference."

"You might not. I would. I'll do my own." She buttered three buns and put them on to toast away from the flame, grilled three hamburgers until they were medium rare and juicy, and then brought them over to Ezra and Dave.

Cathleen watched her laughing and talking with the two men and thought, my how domestic we are all of a sudden. She was perched on a tree stump against the wall of the music barn, spitefully unsociable. Miranda hadn't let her bring the dogs. She transferred her gaze to Roger, and sniffed as she observed the disgraceful exhibition he was making of himself with that blonde child. A bearded tomcat—but he certainly knew how to get around women, and she wouldn't be at all surprised at anything she found out about him. On the other hand, Cathleen reminded herself with some complacency, she was in no position to cast the first stone or make a moral judgment. She closed her eyes, and images of her own past indiscretions drifted through her mind like the opening reels of a vintage Joan Crawford movie until she heard Horace's voice say, "Wake up, sleeping beauty." He was standing in front of her carrying hamburgers and two cans of beer. "At my age," he said, "the prince offers food first."

"As long as I eventually get to be kissed," she answered, and as they laughed together for a moment both of them looked young.

"Come on, Arlene!" Maura Prentice, holding her violin case by its shoulder strap, faced her accusingly. "Nobody else can read well enough to play them without rehearsal. You've got to!"

Arlene glowered back at her, sullen and withdrawn. "No. I don't *have* to do anything. I don't want to play, I've changed my mind."

"Ezra," Maura appealed to him. "Make her. Tell her she's got to play these sonatas with me like she promised. Especially after we rehearsed and everything." Maura was close to tears.

"It's up to Arlene whether she keeps her promise to you and Miranda. No one can force her to play."

"You're all alike, aren't you?" Arlene said angrily. "All so reasonable and rational." Suddenly she capitulated. "Oh all right. I have to warm up anyway."

Ezra smiled and said, "I'll turn for you if you want." She nodded. The three of them walked up the stone ramp of the music barn. Ezra pushed the double-width door open—its grooved wheels rumbled back smoothly on the track—and then flicked on the light switch. With the light on the building became a shallow bright box, a floodlit stage set six feet off the ground on a stone foundation.

The barn had been built originally for horses and hay; all the partitions, including the floor of the hayloft, had long since been ripped out, so that it was now only a rough-finished and sturdily-beamed shell. The walls had been whitewashed inside and out, and the original hardpacked dirt floor had been covered with random-width planks painted dark red. The only other touch of color was the shiny black case of the concert grand

55

gleaming against the white of the walls. Six metal folding chairs were set up in a circle next to the bow of the piano; in front of each chair was an open metal music stand. Over this circle of spindly furniture hung a single large floodlight. An enormous cone fashioned from four lengths of woven bamboo strips lined with white cloth shaded the bulb, focusing the illumination on the music stands and keeping the rest of the barn relatively dim.

Ezra switched on the small piano light and moved four of the chairs and five of the music stands back against the wall. One of the chairs he left where it was, with its music stand, under the spotlight for Maura; the other he moved a little to the left and in back of the piano bench, so he could sit there and be ready to turn the pages of Arlene's music. While he was setting up, Arlene sat slumped over on the piano bench striking *A* with one finger for Maura's tuning, looking totally bored.

Horace stuck his head in the door and said, "All set, me proud beauties?" Maura sighed and nodded, Arlene nodded. They conferred and agreed in a few low words about tempos and repeats, then each sat up straight and assumed a serious expression. Outside Horace picked up a big stone and banged it against a clapperless iron bell screwed to the barn wall.

"Music! Hey everybody, listen! Maura and Arlene will now play."

He went back to the beer tub, then over to where Cathleen was waiting for him. The rest of the group took a couple of minutes to settle down in the grass in front of the open door, light cigarettes, arrange themselves. Somebody yelled, "What are they going to play?"

Miranda said in a low, clear schoolmistress voice, "Girls, announce your program."

Arlene looked at Maura and said, "You." Maura got up, walked quickly to the door, took a step down the ramp and said in a loud excited voice, "We're going to do two Mozart sonatas, K 306 and 304, in D and E minor." Someone cheered, someone else groaned. Maura ran back to her chair and sat down, then bobbed up again and added, "We're doing 304 first I meant to say." She finally settled herself, looked at Arlene, poised her bow over the violin strings, gave the down-beat by nodding her head, and they were off. Both of them were good musicians, expert enough to make the sonatas, for all their predictability of form and development, excitingly spontaneous music. K 304, a melancholy and reflective piece, was greeted by prolonged applause; K 306, with its final brilliant allegro, by bravos. Maura, flushed and pleased, took her bows, stretched her young body unselfconsciously, and went out to join the audience. Ezra came out front and sat where he could watch Arlene's face.

The group took a few minutes to quiet down again. Arlene waited until they were all settled, then rose, advanced across the wine-dark floor, and announced clearly into the now complete summer darkness, "I shall play the Chopin Scherzo in B minor, Opus 20." She walked back to the piano, sat down, closed her eyes for a second, flexed her fingers, held her hands over the keyboard, and crashed down into the first chords.

Ezra was astounded. He knew from the way she'd read through the sonatas that she had terrific facility, but he was nonetheless completely unprepared for such virtuosity in someone her age. Apart from having the technique to surmount Chopin's formidable require-ments, she knew, she had grasped entirely, what his music meant and was communicating her knowledge. Her interpretation, the reasoned application of tech-nique to content, was a lecture, a discourse on the

57

meaning of rebellion and consequent disenchantment, a declaration of astonished betrayal and heroically angry despair. When she finished—the final rapid crescendos played with unbelievable power and intensity—she received the ovation she deserved. In response to the clapping and yelling she got up and bowed just once, then sat down again. Ezra saw she was trembling and called to her softly, "Arlene? Are you all right?" She looked at him, her ashen face a mute appeal. She needs help, he thought, I'd better—But before he was even halfway out of his chair, Roger had come bounding up the ramp and gotten between them. He knelt before her, took her hands in his, and kissed them. "Magnificent," he said, "you were magnificent."

Most of the other students followed Roger into the barn, crowding around the piano, noisily congratulating her. Ezra tried to push his way through to her, but again Roger thwarted him. He put his arm around Arlene's shoulders and pulled her up off the bench. Raising his voice above the clamor he cried, "Everybody—come on up to my cabin. I'm going to give a real party in honor of Arlene."

Half-supporting her, half-dragging her, her hand locked firmly in his own, he led her out into the night.

7

The morning after the picnic, as soon as Miranda had done everything she had to in the office, she headed for the potting shed. Janice was already there, laboriously mashing tiny pieces of clay together, building up a formless sculpture over a wire armature. She looked up when Miranda came in and waved a silent hello, to which Miranda replied with an equally wordless nod. Going over to the clay barrel, she reached down into it with both hands, scooped out a great hunk of stiff red clay, and spent the next hour wedging it to the right consistency and trying to throw all of it into a single pot. The ball of clay was too big for her to work with easily, and in between the times when she was absorbed in her own work, Janice watched her struggling with it, fascinated by her stubborn and somehow ferocious insistence on doing what she'd set her mind to. She finally managed to get the clay under control, after having to start over twice, and then rapidly threw it into a large, graceful tureen. When she was finally satisfied, she pried the batt off the wheelhead and put it, with the tureen attached, on the counter.

Janice looked up. "That's a very nice pot, Miranda."

"Thanks." Miranda pushed her hair back off her forehead, leaving a smudge of clay up the side of her face. "I'll have to make the handles tomorrow; it took more time than I thought it would." She washed her hands and sat down opposite Janice. "That's much better."

"What is?"

"Me. I'm not so tense."

"Yes, it's very satisfactory for that." Janice frowned at her sculpture and pushed the mass a little away from her. "Cigarette?" She held the pack out. Miranda took one and lit hers and Janice's, and they sat there wordlessly, involved in their own thoughts. Then, Cathleen came striding up and paused at the shed door.

"Miranda! Thank heavens!"

"What's the matter?" Cathleen's voice was so urgent that Miranda automatically responded with alarm.

"Have you seen Arlene this morning?"

"Is that all you want?" Miranda ground her half-smoked cigarette out on the floor beneath her shoe.

"No."

Cathleen came forward, her hands behind her back. "Neither have I, and I've been looking for her all over."

"She's practicing in her cabin."

"No, she's not. I went up there to see."

"Maybe," Janice suggested, her voice tonelessly noncommittal, "she's at Roger's cabin."

"Nonsense, why would she be there?" Janice shrugged. "Besides," Miranda added, "today's Tuesday. He left for Northampton early this morning."

"Then maybe she went with him."

"Never mind Roger," Cathleen leaned over them. "I'm not looking for him, it's her! I can't find her, and I can't find anybody who's seen her this morning, either." The last part of the sentence was a horrified whisper.

"Will you stop this ridiculous melodrama," Miranda said angrily, "and tell me what this is all about?"

"It's not melodrama. Look!" Cathleen stood tall and brought her hands around so that they could see what she was holding.

"What is it?" Miranda still refused to be impressed.

"It's Arlene's blouse—the one she was wearing last night."

"Arlene's blouse! Let me see that!" Miranda grabbed for it and turned it over, inspecting it. "How do you know it's hers? Why is it so dirty? Where'd you find it?"

"That's just it," Cathleen said, "I didn't. It could've been anywhere. Woglinda found it and brought it back to me from someplace, but I can't get her to tell me where. And I'm sure it's Arlene's—look, that little cameo she always wears is still pinned to the collar."

The three women gazed at the piece of dirty white fabric, until Miranda, rousing herself, said, "Very well,

I'll find out about it."

She and Cathleen went over to the dormitory, a converted farmhouse, and upstairs to Arlene's room. It was in perfect order. Either the bed hadn't been slept in at all, or it had already been made earlier in the morning. They looked around helplessly for a minute, then Miranda went out and knocked on the door of the adjoining bedroom.

"Come in," a sleepy voice said.

"Maura, are you still in bed?" Miranda asked, opening the door.

"Uh huh," Maura yawned.

"How well do you know what clothes Arlene has?"

"Pretty well, we wear the same size," Maura said, sitting up and reaching for her glasses. Putting them on, she asked interestedly, "What's the matter?"

"Nothing's the matter. Do you know if this is hers?" Miranda shook out the blouse and held it up. Maura hopped out of bed and came across the room barefoot. She held the blouse up, scrutinizing it.

"Yes, I think so, she was wearing it last night. That's her pin, anyway."

"Come in here, will you? Put a robe and slippers on first," Maura looked surprised, but obeyed meekly. "Hi, Cathleen," she said, following Miranda into Arlene's bedroom.

"Good morning." Cathleen was sitting in the one chair, part spectator, part actor.

"Would you look through her closet and see if you can tell if anything's missing—if any other clothes're gone?"

"What, has she run out?"

"I'll explain later," Miranda said firmly. "Please, just do as I ask you."

Maura opened the closet door and pushed slowly through the dresses and blouses. "As far as I can tell," she said, "the only thing that's missing here is a black skirt, the one she was wearing last night. She has three, and the other two are here." She checked the shoe bag hanging on the closet door. "I think all her shoes're here, except those black flats she was wearing yesterday."

"I see."

Maura said, "Excuse me a minute, will you, I have to go to the john. I'll be right back."

"Don't say anything to anybody."

"I won't." She ran out of the room.

"It's a cinch she didn't drive to Northampton with Roger without a blouse on," Cathleen remarked.

Miranda sat down on the bed, her face tense. Maura was back in five minutes, washed and combed, dressed in shorts and a shirt.

"I thought of something," she said excitedly. "Look in her bureau drawer, the second one down, and see if her wallet's there." Miranda pulled out the drawer, both Cathleen and Maura hanging over her shoulder. Maura pointed. "She keeps it under those sweaters." Miranda ran her hands along the bottom of the drawer. "Here it is." She brought out a pigskin wallet, and opened it. It bulged with photos and papers; the money compartment held fifty-two dollars in small bills.

The next couple of hours were spent searching all the school buildings—barns, dormitories, practice cabins, dining hall. Nothing. Together Cathleen and Miranda walked through the pastures around the school, while Horace drove to the village and looked in every single store on Main Street. She wasn't in any of them, and nobody had seen her. When the three of them met on the front lawn after their fruitless searches, Horace rubbed his ruddy jaw and said, "It appears to me, Mandy, we're going to have to call in the gendarmes."

"No!" Miranda was vehement.

"Yes!" Horace insisted. "You wouldn't want Arlene's family to think we hadn't done our best to find her, would you?"

"Couldn't we wait until Roger comes? She may be with him. He's supposed to be back by two or two-thirty."

"She isn't with him, you know that as well as I do. And the less time we waste, the better off we'll be."

"No, I guess she isn't with him." She bit her lip. "You're right, Horace. I suppose we must." She went into the house, and through the open office window they heard her say, in a perfectly calm voice, "Operator, will you please ring the police station in Leesfield for me? Good morning, may I speak to Captain Henderson? Owen? Owen, this is Miranda Boardman at Roundmount School. One of our women students seems to have disappeared. We've searched the whole place and can't find her anywhere. Yes, we're sure. No, we don't know when. Yes, I'm afraid so. Thanks, Owen. We'll wait for you here at the house."

8

Owen put down the phone. "We've got to go up the hill," he said to Mike. "Somebody's missing at Roundmount."

"Male or female?"

"Girl."

Mike made a sceptical noise. "Probably they just can't find where she's shacked up. You know what goes on up there."

"No, I don't think so. Miranda's too level-headed to panic over nothing."

63

"I'll bring Buster in case she's lost in the woods."

"You and that dog!" Owen laughed. "What the hell, why not? But he rides in the back seat. That's an order."

"Okay." Mike shambled out of the room, pulling the knot of his tie up where it belonged. When Owen came out to the police car he got an enthusiastic reception from Buster, who occupied the front seat next to Mike.

"I thought I told you to put him in the back," Owen said as firmly as he could while Buster was licking his face.

"You try keeping him back there," Mike retorted. "I only got two hands, and I need at least one to drive with. I told you before, he likes to see where he's going."

"Look," Owen said, exasperated, still fending the dog off, "do you own him, or does he own you?"

Mike shrugged.

"Get in there, go on—in the back, Buster," Owen ordered, opening the door and pointing to the back seat. The bloodhound stared mournfully at him, drooling a little; then he reluctantly heaved himself out, got into the back, and sat down. "See," Owen said, getting in, "nothing to it. You merely have to show him who's boss."

Mike shrugged again and put the car in gear. As soon as he had it up to forty, Buster started to whine uneasily. Mike moved way over to the left edge of the seat and took a firm grip on the wheel. Suddenly Buster was between them, leaning affectionately against Owen's shoulder and panting hotly into his ear.

"Get away." Owen pushed the dog, a gesture which unfortunately he took as an invitation to play. Shouting didn't help; in the end Mike had to stop the car, get out, run around, open the other door, and pull the dog off Owen's chest. "All right," Owen said, sitting up and dusting himself off, while Mike, laughing helplessly, held Buster on a short leash, "*I'll* get in the back. But it's the last time." He sat there in silent injured dignity all the rest of the way up the mountain. Now and then Buster turned his head around and cast him a benevolent glance.

The police car pulled up in front of the main house. Before they came out of the house to meet Owen, Miranda said to Horace, "I can handle this myself. See what you can do to keep the students out of the way."

"I think I'd better be there," he answered.

She stopped. "No! I can manage Owen by myself, I know him a lot better than you do."

He glared at her, then said, furiously, "Very well, if that's the way you want it." He turned his back on her and began to walk down the hill.

"Where's Horace going?" Owen said to Miranda as she came up to him.

"He has something urgent to take care of," she answered. "Let's talk out here, it's private." She led him through the house out to the back porch. They sat down in the swing, and Owen took notes while she recited the events of the morning.

"Why are you so sure she's not in Northampton?" Owen asked when she was through.

"How could she be? There's her blouse."

"That doesn't mean anything. You can't be sure this blouse and her skirt are all that's missing from her closet. That's the first thing. The second thing is that Maura probably doesn't know exactly what clothes she has. And as far as the dog's finding it is concerned, she could've dropped it anywhere—out of a laundry bag, for instance, in the middle of the road."

Miranda frowned at the ash on her cigarette. "Owen, you know me well enough to know I wouldn't bring you up here for nothing."

"Of course. So far, though, you haven't convinced me there's any real reason for you to be so worried."

"Well, the thing is—"

"Well, what?"

"The thing is," Miranda said a little desperately, "she's not normal, exactly."

"What do you mean, 'not normal exactly'? Stop beating around the bush. What is the matter with her?"

"She's been in an—institution."

"You mean, a mental institution? Are you trying to tell me she's cracked?"

Miranda gave up. "Well, mentally ill, yes. That is, she was. She's better now. I gather she was committed sometime last year. This is all confidential, of course."

"How long as she been out?"

"A couple of months."

"What's she doing here?"

"To tell you the truth, Owen, I didn't know about her problems until after I'd accepted the deposit, and then it was too late. I mean, you can't say to a young girl you're crazy so you can't come here. Besides, she's so gifted I wanted to do anything I could to help her career. You heard her play last night."

"Yes, she's remarkable, no question."

"Her family thought Roundmount would be just right for her, since there's so little pressure."

"They must think she's recovered if they're willing to send her away from home."

"I would assume so. I've never discussed it with them. As a matter of fact they never even mentioned she'd been ill."

"Then how do you know?"

"Horace's cousin Clara Allen works for the father. I never talked to her about it, but he did."

"I see. And Arlene never said anything to you?"

"Not a word. And of course I couldn't bring it up if

she didn't. It would have seemed like prying."

"Okay. Let's see. About five six, weight about 110, very long light-brown hair. Brown eyes?"

"Yes, that's right."

"Any scars or marks?"

"Not that I know of. Why? Are you going to put out some kind of bulletin?"

"Missing person, of course."

"No, not yet. Please."

"Don't you want me to find her?"

"Certainly. But aren't you going to check around here first?"

"Of course I am. It doesn't seem reasonable that she'd start to walk to Leesfield in the middle of the night."

"That's my point, Owen. Supposing she isn't better? That means she isn't reasonable. God knows what she'd do if she's still disturbed. This—" she picked up the blouse—"probably means that she's wandering around here right this minute half naked. You've got to find her before she gets to the village or the main road, before somebody sees her and finds out she's from Round-mount. I don't need that kind of publicity and scandal. It wouldn't be good for Arlene's career, either. Poor girl. It's just awful to think she might be starting to break down again."

"Uh huh." Owen put his notebook away. "Come on, let's see what we can do to save your various reputations."

He led her around the side of the house back to the front lawn. A number of students were there, leaning against the police car, patting Buster, chatting with Mike. They all turned to stare silently at Owen, rather, he thought, like a flock of curious penguins. "Damn," Miranda said under her breath.

"Mike, c'mere a minute, will you?" Mike handed

Buster's leash to one of the students, and came over. Owen explained how Arlene's blouse had been found. "Do you think there's a chance that Buster might be able to find out where it was and track her down? Miranda thinks she's probably not too far away."

Mike was doubtful. "Maybe," he said. "Too many people have handled this to use it, though. Is there something else of hers I could give him?"

"Sure." Owen beckoned one of the girls over. "What's your name?" he asked.

"Debbie."

"Debbie, do you know where Arlene Horowitz's room is?"

She nodded.

"Would you do me a favor and go get one of her blouses out of her closet and bring it back here?"

Without asking for any explanation, Debbie lit out at a dead run. Miranda said sharply, "Why'd you do that? Now they'll all know what's going on."

"They all know now," Owen replied impatiently. "There's no point in trying to keep something like this a secret, you can't do it. Listen." He raised his voice. "Where's whats-her-name, the one whose dog found the blouse?"

"Cathleen—she's at the dining hall—she went to have lunch," four penguins answered in chorus. "Want me to go tell her you want to see her?" one of the boys volunteered. Owen nodded, and he sprinted off down the hill.

"Will this do?" Debbie panted up and held out a blouse. "I took one that isn't very clean, I thought it would smell more like her."

"Good girl." Owen turned away and pretended to examine the blouse so she wouldn't see his grin.

"Here's Cathleen," Miranda said. "Oh, God, she's got those dogs with her."

68

Cathleen was proceeding regally up the road, flanked by the Great Danes. Buster raised his noble head, sighted them, and went flying off to say hello. Luckily the boy holding his leash had a good grip and long legs. The three dogs circled warily in the middle of the road, oblivious to tugs, threats, or commands. Cathleen finally came up by herself, and Miranda introduced her to Owen.

"You don't have any idea where your dog found this blouse?" he asked her.

"Alas, no. As I told Miranda, I just couldn't get her to tell me, either."

Owen scowled. "You didn't happen to see which direction it was coming from?"

"Not it, she." Cathleen thought a minute. "You know," she said, astonished, "that's very clever of you. She must've been coming up the hill, because I can remember, I saw her trot along the driveway to the dining hall and turn off up the hill to go around to the back of the house. She wouldn't've come down the hill from the back and then gone all the way around the front, just to go around to the back again, would she?"

"She might have," Owen replied. "Dogs aren't very bright, you know." Before Cathleen could contradict him, he walked down to Mike, who was still trying to wrestle Buster away from his new playmates.

"There's a good chance that the dog picked it up down the hill from the dining hall. See what you can do, will you?"

Mike nodded. "Come on, Buster," he pleaded, "we got work to do." Somehow he got through to the bloodhound who finally turned serious and deigned to notice the blouse Mike held out to him.

"If you're tracking down something that Woglinda found," Debbie suggested enthusiastically, "wouldn't it be more logical to give him her collar and have him trace *her* trail back to where she found the blouse?"

Mike bristled. "Cut it out," he snapped. "Blood-hounds're very sensitive, and they don't like people laughing at them. Particularly Buster."

"I wasn't laughing," Debbie said, crushed. "I was only trying to be helpful."

"Huh." Mike led Buster away, and the rest of them followed to where the driveway to the dining hall branched off the road. Mike gave the dog the blouse to sniff again; then, tail up, nose down, Buster cast around, tugging at the end of his leash. Suddenly he let out a great bark, and took off, careening full tilt down the hill, almost pulling Mike off his feet after him. A few more students had joined the party, and they all streamed after Mike. Now that he was working, Buster ignored everybody, including the Great Danes, who trotted curiously alongside him, getting in his way. He led them straight along the edge of the road for about a third of a mile, then stopped, cast around again, and found the trail once more.

Expounding the obvious, Mike pointed. "It goes into the woods, down that path," he said.

"Sure it's not a rabbit?" Owen asked, thinking it was hard to tell who was more excited, Buster or Mike.

"It's awful straight for a rabbit track. I think he's really got something."

"Okay." Owen turned to face the students who were crowded at his heels. "This is as far as you go," he said firmly. They groaned a protest. "This isn't a performance, we don't need any audience. Back!"

They retreated grudgingly halfway up the hill, and without exception sat down to wait just in case.

"I'm coming," Cathleen announced flatly.

"All right," Owen said. "But get rid of them." He pointed to the Great Danes. "They'll just be in the way."

Cathleen looked at the dogs and drew herself up. "Hence!" she ordered.

"*Hence*?" Owen echoed, unbelieving.

"Scoot," Cathleen explained in an aside. "But hence reads better, don't you think? It has more authority, somehow."

The dogs whined, protesting in the same tone the students had used. "You heard me, get over there with them." She pointed to the waiting crowd. The dogs turned and paced slowly away, their heads hanging. "Keep them with you," Cathleen shouted, and the kids, laughing and talking among themselves, waved and yelled back.

"See? That's how to make them mind," Owen said. Mike grunted.

"My good man," Cathleen remarked, "if you'd directed as many opera choruses as I have, you'd know how to make them move where you wanted too."

"Come on," Mike said impatiently. "You want Buster t'go cold?" He let out the leash, and Buster tugged him ahead, almost running.

"Where's this path go?" Owen asked as they trotted through the trees after him.

"Parallel with Little River and down," Miranda answered. "I think it comes out down on the main highway just south of Middle Road." She stopped talking and saved her breath for keeping up.

Ahead, Mike shouted. When they caught up to him, he pointed to a fallen pine tree. A black skirt lay neatly folded on its trunk. Owen picked it up and shook it out. "This hers?" He asked. Miranda looked at it and said weakly, "I think so."

Owen refolded the skirt and put it back exactly where he'd found it. "Let's go." He abandoned the women and stayed with Mike and the dog, urging them on. In the next fifteen minutes they came across Arlene's slip, bra, and pants, each garment neatly folded and placed right by the side of the trail. With each find, Owen's face got grimmer.

"Hold it." Buster had brought them into a clearing through the middle of which a shallow sun-dappled stream flowed silently on its stony bed. Mike pointed. "Look."

"I see." Owen walked over and stared down at the shoes, set side by side on the river bank with the toes pointing downstream.

"What's in them?" Mike craned his neck.

"Two small tortoiseshell combs and an elastic band." Owen prowled uneasily around the clearing.

"Jesus, she's running around up here without any clothes on at all," Mike said, a mixture of awe and anticipation in his voice. "I sure hope we find her pretty soon." Owen gave him a sour look. "Well, I mean," Mike said, grinning, "you wouldn't want her to stay out too long and catch cold, would you?"

"Where the hell are those two?" Owen muttered, ignoring him. "Oh, here they come."

"Why, this is where we go swimming," Miranda said, looking around. "Though usually we come in that way." And she pointed to another trail running in from their right.

"Does this water get any deeper?"

"Why, no, just at the potho—" Her voice trailed off. "Down there," she whispered. "On the other side of the big boulder."

"Wait here, all of you," Owen commanded. He ran down the bank and disappeared around a curve where the river made a sharp turn to the left.

"*Mike*!"

He swiftly knotted Buster's leash around the stem of a small tree. "You, Buster—sit!" he ordered. "You, too, you stay here with him." He plunged away.

"Holy Mary." Arlene's naked body lay in the water, her legs stretched out downstream, knees resting on the bottom; her torso floated in the middle of the pothole, face down; her outspread hair moved very slightly in the current of the whirlpool.

"Let's get her out of there." Mike squatted beside him on the bank. "I'll bring her shoulders in first, then you take her legs."

Owen reached out and gripped Arlene's left wrist, and tugged at it, lifting it slightly out of the water as he pulled her body toward him. The wrist felt wrong, somehow—it was too limp, as though it was unconnected. And then, as her elbow came out of the water, he suddenly, shockingly, saw why. Most of the inside of her upper arm was missing. A great ragged-edged hole gaped between her elbow and her armpit, a wound so deep and huge that almost the entire bone shone bare. Thin frayed strips of skin and flesh hung off the edge of it, waving back and forth like tendrils in the water.

"Jesus, look at that, what the hell happ—" Mike looked and made a noise as if he'd been punched in the stomach. Owen grasped the backs of her shoulders and lifted. As her face came out of the water, the snapping turtle that had been gnawing at it sank away into the opaque depths of the pool. A piece of her eyeball fell out and floated down slowly after it. She had only half a head—the right side was eaten away almost down to the skull.

"Pull her out of there, quick." Mike grabbed her waist, and together they lifted the upper half of the corpse free of the water. Two other snappers, one on her breast, the other feeding deep inside a great hole in her abdomen, alerted by the previous tugging, had clamped their jaws in time. They swung there, long tails flailing, leathery dark legs clawing to brace themselves

73

against the pale flesh, malevolent hooked beaks clenched tight, prepared to hang there forever.

"Get them off, get them off!"

"Hold her up!" Owen ordered in a harsh whisper. Unable to believe what he had to do, refusing to understand it, he reached around to his back pocket for his knife and opened it. "Hold her *up*, I said!" One hand grabbed the tail of the turtle whose head was inside her, and pulled at it. The neck came out, festooned with a loop of entrail. He tugged, but the turtle had such a firm hold inside that he couldn't shake its head free.

"Won't it come out? Make it come out!"

"I'll have to—" Owen held the turtle's body out as far and as straight as he could, gritted his teeth, and plunged his knife into its neck, just above the leathery carapace. Mike barely stifled his cry as the blood spurted out. The legs paddled desperately, and the body squirmed as Owen sawed through its flesh as fast as he could, his knife blade squeaking against the rubbery wet skin. But the jaws never budged. Even after Owen had severed the body and hurled it violently up on the bank, the head was right where it had been when he started— inside, with the jaws closed. Owen started to reach into the hole in her stomach to pull it out, then whispered hoarsely, "I can't, I can't," and closed his throat against waves of nausea.

When the spasms had passed, he said, "You'll have to hold her higher so I can get the other one off." Shuddering with disgust, Mike clutched at Arlene's body and dragged it up until her back lay against his chest. Her head lolled forward, and her hair mercifully fell over and hid what was left of her face. Owen grabbed the other turtle, and cut it off by slicing through the hinge of Arlene's flesh that held it to her body.

"They're both off. Drag her out."

74

Mike opened his eyes. Owen still gripped the second turtle by one of its back legs. A flap of Arlene's skin dangled obscenely out of its mouth, draped back against the shell. Dropping the knife, Owen grabbed the other back leg, stood up, and held the turtle out, almost horizontally. Hissing, it retracted its head as far as it could, then shot it out again and again in vicious lunging attacks, snapping fiercely at the air. Its front legs paddled the air like grotesque webbed oars, and its leathery body with its incomplete shell twisted frantically in Owen's grip. He swung it over his head, and with a tremendous thwack slammed it down against a flat boulder, cracking its armor; kneeling, he battered at it furiously with a rock until its plastron had splintered and shreds of bloody turtle meat and shell were splattered over the bank, pounding at it until, swearing and trembling, and close to tears, he was satisfied he'd destroyed it utterly.

He stood up and looked around. Mike was arranging his coat over Arlene's body to hide as much as he could.

"Are you all right?"

"I guess so. You?"

"Yeah." He took a deep breath and wiped his forehead on the sleeve of his jacket. "I hope I never—" He became aware that somebody was behind him, and whirled. Miranda and Cathleen stood there, transfixed. Both men at once stepped between them and the body. Miranda looked at the headless turtle at her feet and put her hand to her mouth. "She's dead?"

"That's right." Owen moved toward her, then stopped. He saw his knife lying on the bank and bent to pick it up, watching as if from a great distance the way his hand shook as he snapped it shut. Cathleen said, "Come, Miranda, we'll go back now."

Only by making a great and deliberate effort could Owen resume his role of authority. "Go with them,

Mike. Call Frank Burch and see if you can reach Dawson. Use the other path, it's probably shorter, we must be pretty close to the road here. Then come back, I'll wait."

Mike began to shepherd the women ahead of him. Buster barked as they came around the curve, and Mike went over to him, knelt to untie the leash, and hugged him. The dog whimpered and licked his face. The four of them moved slowly out of the clearing, Cathleen and Miranda clinging to one another, Mike holding Buster close to his leg on a tight lead.

Left to himself, Owen lit a cigarette and took a deep drag. He looked at his hands. They were filthy and wet, covered with leaves and dirt and blood. He sniffed them—they smelled foul and musky. He plodded stiff-legged back up to the clearing, stripped off his jacket, took off his wristwatch—it was exactly two forty-five, he noticed—and rolled up his shirtsleeves. Paying great attention to what he was doing, he carefully washed his hands and arms in the water; wetting his handkerchief, he sponged the spots off the front of his pants as best he could. Then he sat down—not near Arlene's body, but where he could keep an eye on it—and waited for Mike to come back, summoning his resources for whatever might lie ahead. Now and then he could hear a turtle surface for air, gulp, and slide down again into the muddy depths of the pool.

9

In a little while Owen heard car doors slam, and Mike's voice saying, "In here, Doc." He got to his feet and walked to the edge of the clearing to greet them. Frank

Burch looked around. "Mike's told me what you found . . . Where is she?"

Owen pointed, and the three of them walked down the bank. Burch slid Mike's coat off her and made a shocked sound. "Isn't that awful," he said. "So young." He dropped the coat back on top of her, and stood up. "I brought a stretcher and blankets with me," he said, "they're in the back of the station wagon."

They wrapped the body in the blankets, and rolled it onto the stretcher, carried it out to the car, and slid her in over the tailgate.

"When can I have a report?" Owen asked.

"Soon as I get it done. She'll wait—my live patients won't."

"By tomorrow?"

"I'll try, but I can't promise anything. If Mike's cousin Gloria decides to have her baby tonight, the way she's supposed to, I'll have to let it go till after."

"You'll be able to get it done with no trouble," Mike promised him. "Gloria's always late to everything."

Burch drew Owen to one side. "Do you feel all right? You look pretty rocky."

"Yeah, I'm okay, I'm not used to—" He waved his hand toward the station wagon. "Not like that, anyway." He added, finally able to think about it, "You know, there's a turtle head inside, I just couldn't get it out of her."

"Don't worry, I'll cut it out. Something ought to be done about those goddam animals." He opened the car door. "I almost forgot, here's your lawful fifty cents, Mike," and he held out two quarters.

Mike took them. "Of all the dumb things—"

"Legally I have to pay you for reporting a dead body to the medical examiner, and you know it as well as I do. I'll call you as soon as I'm through." He waved and was gone.

"Did you get in touch with Dawson?" Owen asked.

"Yep. Do we wait for him here?"

"No reason to. Let's get over to Miranda's house and see what's going on."

Mike slung his wet jacket on the back seat and started the car. "Hold it," Owen said, "Somebody's coming." A red sports car with its top down went by, jouncing up the ruts. The driver stared at them curiously through his wrap-around sunglasses.

"Hurry up," Owen ordered. "That must be Benton."

Mike turned out into the road. "Shall I pull him over?"

"No, let him go."

They passed the place where Arlene had turned off the road. A little further up, about a dozen students were still sitting together, talking. Roger saw them. He peered in the mirror at the police car, and without signaling, pulled off the road and skidded to a stop on the grass.

"Alison," he called. "What's going on?"

Mike pulled up in back of him. Owen opened the car door and stepped out to observe.

Two of the girls detached themselves from the group and walked slowly over to Roger.

"It's Arlene—"

"What about her? What'd she do?" He grabbed her arm.

"She's—" Alison hesitated and looked over at Owen, who returned her glance impassively.

"She's dead."

"Dead? How?" Roger shook her arm.

"Ouch," she protested, and pulled away from him. "*How*?"

"I don't know. Drowned, Cathleen said."

Without another word Roger threw the car into gear

78

and roared off. Everybody watched the car zoom up the hill past the main house, turn left off the road, and stop in front of a small cabin. Roger got out and ran into the house. The sharp crack of the door slamming behind him drifted down the hill a few seconds after he'd disappeared inside.

"That his cabin?" Owen asked.

The girls nodded. Alison was still rubbing her wrist.

Up at the main house they met Cathleen in the hall on her way to the kitchen. She was carrying a tray with a cup and saucer on it.

"Where's Miranda?" Owen asked.

"Upstairs in bed, resting. I just gave her a cup of tea with some whiskey in it. She'll be all right in a little while." Cathleen looked at them. "It wouldn't hurt you to have a drink, either."

"I could use a cup of coffee," Owen admitted, and Mike agreed.

"Come on in the kitchen, I made a big pot just in case. I knew somebody'd drink it." She got out the cups and found some cookies, and the three of them sat at the round oilcloth covered kitchen table, sipping the hot liquid.

"Wonder where Horace is," Owen said. "You'd think—"

"Don't blame Horace," Cathleen said waspishly. "Miranda probably sent him off someplace. Too afraid he might want to have something to say about what's going on."

Owen raised an eyebrow, but before he could pursue the subject further, rapid footsteps sounded on the back porch, and two men appeared in the doorway.

"Cathleen," one of them began, "what's happened? We just this minute—" He saw the uniforms. "Owen, I'm Ezra Agnew. We met last night."

"Yes, of course. Hi, Dave."

79

Cathleen said, "Coffee?"

"Please." Ezra sat down. "Tell me," he said to Owen, "what's happened? Is it true that Arlene's dead?"

"Yes."

"Suicide." It was not a question.

"How come you're so sure?"

"She was a pretty sick kid," Ezra said, stirring his coffee. "She should never've been released so soon. If she'd been my patient—"

"How did you know she'd been hospitalized? Did you know her before?"

"No, certainly not. She told me herself that she'd been treated for a schizophrenic breakdown. She boasted to me that she was all better. Of course she wasn't, and she knew it."

"When did she tell you this?"

"Yesterday. We hadn't had much to say to one another before then. She showed up at the studio in the afternoon with some irrelevant questions about painting. Just an excuse to start talking with me. It didn't take much before she was telling me what was really on her mind."

"Which was?"

"That she needed help. Not," Ezra added bitterly, "that I helped her, apparently."

"There's no reason to reproach yourself," Cathleen put in. "You couldn't possibly have changed anything by one conversation."

"Perhaps not. But she'd asked me for help, and to that extent I failed her."

"Did you know anything about this?" Owen asked Dave.

"Not a thing. I don't think I spoke to the poor girl more than to say hi. I only get to know the art students. Of course I heard her play last night."

"And you?"

Cathleen shook her head. "I went riding with her a couple of times before the rest of the students came up, but I never talked to her much about herself."

"Did she have any good friends among the students?"

"I don't know, but I don't think so. You'd have to ask them. Maybe Maura Prentice, since they played together."

"What'd Benton have to do with her?"

"Nothing," Miranda's voice said strongly. She came into the kitchen with her usual assured stride.

"Feel better?" Cathleen asked.

"I'm all right." She poured herself a cup of coffee, and came over to the table. "Ezra," she said, "I'm going to ask you a favor."

"What is it?"

"I want you to call Arlene's parents and tell them what's happened."

"Me? Why me? I don't even know who they are."

"Please. You're a doctor, you'll know how to break it to them. It's going to be such a shock for them."

Ezra considered a minute, then shook his head decisively. "No, Miranda. I can't accept that responsibility."

"Very well." The hand holding her coffee cup trembled, but she didn't protest his refusal. Cathleen looked down at the table and sniffed.

The front doorbell rang, and a state trooper walked in without being invited. "Hi, Al," Owen said. He and Mike got up and went to meet him.

"Owen, Mike. What's going on?"

"Out here would be better," Owen said, and the three of them went outside. In a few minutes Owen put his head in the door and said, "Dr. Agnew, will you come with me, please?"

81

Ezra finished his coffee and got up. Outside, Mike and the trooper were getting into the state patrol car. They drove off down the hill.

"Where're they going?" Ezra asked.

"To pick up the clothes."

"What clothes?"

"I forgot, you don't know about that. Come on across the street and I'll tell you." They sat facing each other on two flat, moss-covered rocks. Ezra listened carefully while Owen recited how they'd found Arlene, although he omitted most of the details about the turtles. At the end, Ezra said, "It fits in."

"What?"

"She told me she used to run away at night. That kind of wandering episode is usually like an SOS, something to draw attention, to make others concerned."

"But if she'd behaved like this before, why should she kill herself this time?"

"I couldn't tell you. Perhaps it was an accident. Was it possible that she slipped and fell in?"

"The bank's no steeper there by the pothole than it is anywhere else along that stream. No. Suicide is right, I think. Those clothes—leaving them like that—it reminded me of Hansel and Gretel, as though she were marking her trail, either for somebody else to follow her and look for her, or maybe even to be able to find her own way back again. Of course, there's the chance that somebody followed her into the woods to kill her, and then threw her in the pothole, hoping the turtles would pick her clean. Or somebody found her wandering in the woods and killed her."

Ezra sighed and shrugged.

"Do you know of anything that happened to her recently that might've pushed her over the edge again?"

"It's hard for me to say," Ezra answered. "I don't know anything about how she felt toward men or sex."

"What does that mean?"

"You remember last night after the concert, when Benton announced that party in his cabin?"

"Yes, but I had to leave right after the music, so I don't know what happened at it. I wouldn't have gone anyway, I don't know Benton at all."

"He took Arlene with him."

"Yes, I saw that. He really swept her off."

"I'm not sure she wanted him to do that. It's not that he forced her exactly, but he's an imperious man, quite powerful and aggressive, and he just sort of carried her along with him. She didn't exactly fight it, but my feeling is she was certainly ambivalent about him. Anyway, I—it was a difficult position for me. I wasn't her doctor, I'm up here on vacation, there wasn't any reason why I had to feel protective or responsible. But still, I didn't like the idea of his taking her off like that, particularly after our conversation in the afternoon. So Jan and I went up there for a little while. It was pretty obvious that Roger had his eye on her, and later on, I thought, she might not be able to get away from him. And of course, like all those ambivalent situations, she probably wasn't absolutely sure she wanted to say no. Sort of like a snake and a bird. I asked her to leave with us, but she refused. Yet I was sure she knew if she didn't get out of there in time she was going to have to face an awkward situation. Maybe she was experienced enough sexually not to think it'd be awkward, but I don't think so. Anyway," he drew a deep breath, "I couldn't force her to leave. But I'd guess that if there was anything—anything recent, that is—that could've precipitated an episode like this, where she'd run away again or contemplate killing herself—from what I was able to observe of her, I'd say it probably'd have something to do with facing the kind of aggression, both sexual and social, that Roger represents."

83

"But she wouldn't leave?"

"No. But don't forget, she wasn't healthy enough to be able to help herself."

"So you think that Benton had something to do with her death?"

"No, no, I didn't say that." Ezra shook his head. "I thought I hedged enough to make that clear. I don't know that anything happened between them, or that Roger even got around to making a pass at her, or that she would've been disturbed by it if he had. I don't know enough about her, and I'm not going to make any accusations like that on the amount of information I have. I can only tell you what *I* saw and how *I* felt, right now. You'll have to find out what actually happened."

"Don't worry, I will." He stood up. Ezra stayed seated, chewing glumly on a piece of grass. "Why did you refuse to call her parents for Miranda?"

Ezra looked up at him. "I don't mind being useful," he said, "but I don't like being used, and that's what Miranda was trying to do, use me. What she wanted was for me to call Arlene's family and identify myself as a psychiatrist, so that they'd think I was involved with Arlene here at the camp, and they'd have somebody to put the blame on besides the Boardmans and themselves. What she wanted me to do is let her assure the parents—and herself, too—that because I was here, and I couldn't stop her from suiciding for all my so-called professional qualifications, that nobody could've."

"But she knows you didn't treat Arlene."

"She knows it now, but if I'd made that call for her, you can bet that pretty soon she'd be thinking I had." He stood up, his face grim. "Maybe there was something I could've done to help her and didn't. All right, to that extent I do share the responsibility for her death, and I have to make my own peace with it. But if her parents ought to feel guilty, or if Miranda should—and believe me, I can hardly conceive that they all shouldn't —why should I contribute to their peace of mind by letting them transfer some of it to me? What the hell was a poor sick kid like that doing out of the hospital? And who set her loose to fend for herself in a place like this where nobody cares what you do?"

"I see. Who's this Jan you mentioned?"

"Janice Hoskins."

"Redhead?"

"Yes."

"She was at the party."

"That's right."

Owen checked the time. It was four-fifteen. "I've got to get going. Thanks for your help." He got into his car and began to drive toward Roger's cabin. A car passed him. The driver tooted his horn, waved, and they both stopped, their front windows opposite.

"Martin."

"Hi, Owen. What're you doing up here?"

"I'm on official business. Unfortunately."

"What's wrong?"

"A young woman was found drowned this afternoon."

"How awful. Who?"

"Arlene Horowitz."

"No! I can't believe it. She played only last night. It's impossible!"

"Did you know her well?"

"I'd seen her a couple of times." He put his head down on the steering wheel and closed his eyes. "I simply cannot believe she's dead."

Owen looked at Martin's pallor and thought, for somebody who didn't know her well you're awfully damned upset, particularly for you. Aloud he said, "Pull over, Martin, and let's talk about it for a

85

minute.''

Martin maneuvered his car off to the side of the road, and Owen walked over and got into the front seat.

"Where did it—where did you find her?"

"In the brook. That pothole."

"With the turtles?"

"Uhhuh."

"Had they—" Owen nodded.

"Ugh." Martin took out his handkerchief and wiped his face. "I've told Mandy a thousand times she ought to clean them out of there, and so has everybody else."

"Tell me what Arlene was like."

"I don't—in what respect?"

"Did she strike you as an especially unhappy girl, for instance? Or maybe upset or very emotional?"

"Unhappy? I really couldn't say, we didn't talk about any—" He closed his eyes on the picture of Arlene crouched on the floor of his cabin and sobbing. "No," he whispered, "we never talked about anything personal."

"You have no idea then why she might commit suicide, what it was that might have been bothering her?"

"Suicide? You mean it wasn't an accident? Didn't she go swimming and drown by accident?"

"It's too early to say for sure, but there are a couple of reasons to think she might've killed herself."

"Oh lord, how horrible it would be if I—to think she killed—" He wiped his face again.

"When did you talk to her last?"

"I can't remember, some day this week—only yesterday, was it yesterday? She was taking a walk and stopped by the house to say hello when she saw I was there. And then I saw her again last night at the picnic and heard her play, but I didn't talk to her then." His voice got louder. "Ask Roger, why don't you? He took her away with him to his cabin last night. Maybe he could explain why she'd want to kill herself."

"Take it easy, Martin." Martin looked at Owen's face and thought he'd better be careful, or Owen would think he was hysterical. He tried to keep his hands from shaking by clasping them tightly together.

"You didn't go to Roger's party?"

"No. We don't get along. He's a hateful, vulgar, dirty man.".

Owen looked at his watch. "I was on my way up to see him, I guess there's still time." He slapped Martin lightly on the shoulder. "Take it easy," he said again, and went back to his own car and rode up to the cabin, parking behind Roger's car. He knocked on the cabin door. No answer. He knocked again and then a third time. No response. He went around to one of the windows and peered in. The cabin looked empty, but it was so dark inside he couldn't be sure. He got as close as possible to the glass and cupped his hands around his eyes so that he could see into the interior. It was an extremely untidy room. Behind him a voice said, sneeringly, "I hate to dash cold water on your high hopes, Peeping Tom, but there's nobody in there. You're wasting your time and your eyesight. And your libido."

Owen turned around slowly. Roger stared back up at him, truculent and alert. Swallowing his anger, Owen said, "Are you looking for a hard time, sonny? If so, you've come to exactly the right place."

"I don't care for spies, public or private."

"And I don't like a smart ass."

"Nobody does, so I've heard." Roger smiled in a way that failed to be disarming. "I saw you at the party last night, but we didn't meet. I'm Roger Benton."

Owen ignored both the smile and the outstretched hand. "I'm Chief Henderson of the Leesfield police.

I'm investigating the death of Arlene Horowitz.''

"Can't tell you a thing about it," Roger said promptly. "I just learned about it a couple of minutes ago, you saw the whole thing. I've been away from school since before seven this morning."

"So I understand. How convenient for you, isn't it?"

"What do you mean by that?"

"How well did you know Miss Horowitz?"

"I met her about two weeks ago, the first day I was here. We had dinner together a few times at Mandy's house before the dining room opened. After it did, I saw her maybe ten times altogether, mostly just in passing. You could scarcely call us old friends."

"That's not surprising. I doubt if you could call anybody an old friend."

"Now see here, officer," Roger began, his temper slipping out of control.

"I understand," Owen cut in calmly, "that she was a guest at your house at a party last night after her performance."

"My, word does get around the social circles here, doesn't it?"

"Yes or no?"

"Yes."

"Did her behavior seem strange?"

Roger started to answer, then changed his mind and closed his mouth.

"Well?"

"Not specially, no."

Owen looked at his watch and abruptly turned his back. "I'll want to talk to you," he said over his shoulder as he moved away, "so don't get any ideas about spending tomorrow someplace else."

"Don't y'all worry, sheriff," Roger called after him. "Any time y'want t'come gunnin' fer me, Ah'll be here.

An' Ah'll even help ya count t'three, in case you f'git how."

"What'd you find out?" Owen asked.

Dr. Burch tossed him a piece of paper. "It's all there." He sat down and busied himself lighting his pipe while Owen read the report. When he was through, he said thoughtfully, "Are you positive?"

"Fairly. I got to her right away yesterday afternoon, but she'd been in the water, don't forget, for eight or nine hours, maybe more. But between my autopsy and the pathologist's report, you ought to have enough evidence to stand up in court."

"Which is all I need." Owen sighed and rubbed the back of his neck. "Oh, Lord, what a rotten mess."

"Isn't it?" Burch puffed a couple of times, then blew out a cloud of smoke. "I know one thing, Owen," he said forcefully, "I'd be damned if I'd send any daughter of mine up there."

"I wouldn't either, but it's probably not as simple as that." Owen swiveled around in his chair so that he faced out the window. The police station was housed on the ground floor of a shingled imitation Richardson building, and the Gothic window, through which he was gazing so gloomily, commanded a view of most of Main Street. As he stared out, he saw Horace Boardman walk across the street two blocks down and go into Ye Olde Colonial Liquor Store. He swiveled back and repeated, "No, it isn't quite so simple."

"What's so goddam difficult, may I ask?" the older

man said sarcastically. "A young girl with her whole life before her gets raped and then goes and drowns herself in a pothole full of scavenging turtles. The issues seem fairly clear cut to me."

"You're sure you can say she was raped? After all, neither of us was there."

"What's the matter, you don't like that word? Then let me remind you of a few details." Burch cleared his throat. "Her physical condition makes it impossible for me to believe she co-operated with her—seducer, if that's what you want to call him. Those bruises on her arms, legs, and throat indicate she was handled very roughly. Stretch it a little, which under the circumstances I am perfectly willing to do, and you could say she was beaten up. The entrance to her vagina was torn and bloody, and semen and blood were present, mixed together, inside. Whatever you call what happened to her, it must've been goddam painful, since the indications are that until last night she was a virgin. And it was probably much more painful than it had to be because she was entered so forcibly and consequently badly torn. Now, does that sound any better than raped?"

"No," Owen admitted, "it doesn't. There's no chance she couldn've gotten those bruises, say, from hitting herself on trees in the dark?"

"Not unless those trees had four fingers and a thumb," Burch answered. "Her right upper arm shows five bruises—four on the outside, one on the inside, that have to've been made by somebody's hand. And that other one, on the inside of her thigh—a big round one—would've been almost impossible for her to give herself unless she stood on one leg and whacked the inside of the other with a stick. It's pretty plain that somebody either kicked her or kneed her. And hard enough," he added, "so that if she were still alive, she'd have a goddam painful time walking today."

"Okay, okay." Owen pulled a manila folder out of his desk drawer, inked a rubber stamp, and stamped *Temporary Coroner's File* across the front of it, filled in the date, wrote *Arlene Horowitz* on the tab, and slipped the report inside.

Miranda wasn't in the office when he got there, nor anyplace in the house. Owen went out the back door and down the path to the potting shed. She wasn't there, either, but a slim redhead was, unwinding a long wet cloth from an amorphous mound of clay. An acrid odor filled the shed.

"Good morning. Miss Hoskins, isn't it?"

"Good morning. You're Owen Henderson, I know."

"Have you seen Miranda?"

"She's in a faculty meeting over at the dining lodge. They started about ten minutes ago."

He grimaced. "They'll be out in less than an hour," she added.

"Well, there's no point in disturbing her. I have to talk to a lot of people this morning, and I'll do that first. Can you stop what you're doing and answer a few questions?"

"Yes, surely. Just let me get some water and sprinkle this first, so it doesn't dry out." She picked up an enamel pan and went over to the sink. He watched her cross the room with interest and approval. "Be careful where you sit down," she said through the rush of the water hitting the pan. "Those chairs are full of clay."

"So I see." He stood until she came back, then sat down opposite her.

"What is it?"

"What, this?" She dipped a rubber bulb fitted with a sprinkler stopper in the pan, and filled it, then started to spray the clay. "It's eventually going to be a kneeling figure, but right now it isn't much of anything. I have to

91

build it up a lot more before I can start working on it.''

"What do you do when you work on it?"

"First I sculpt the figure out of this solid mass, and then dig out most of the inside so that I have a hollow clay shell about an inch thick. Then the shell gets fired in the kiln, and when it comes out I can decide whether or not I like the piece well enough to want to pour it in bronze. If I do, I'll make a cast from the clay figure by covering it with plaster, cut the plaster in half, strip it off, clamp the halves together into a mold, and pour the bronze in. When it's solidified, and the plaster's removed, there's a metal piece that's a replica of the clay model. That has to be smoothed and polished and given a patina, and that's it. It's not as immediate or spontaneous a method as the lost-wax process, but at least you get more chance to think about it than you do when you go into metal right away."

"Do I smell vinegar?"

"It's on that cloth. It keeps the clay from getting too moldy."

"What's the lost-wax process?"

"It's—" Janice stopped and put her sprinkler down. "You didn't come in to get lectured on sculpture techniques. I thought you had work to do?"

"Sure I do, but I like the way you lecture."

She took a good look at him, and liked what she saw: a big solid man, with an air of intelligent purpose and great competence.

"Want me to stand up and flex my muscles for you?" he asked, grinning confidently under her inspection. "I'm six three, I weigh 173, I'm single, and I'm in excellent physical condition."

"No, you don't have to bother standing up, I can see quite well what you're like sitting down." She smiled. "If you don't mind my asking, what's a beautiful doll like you doing in a dump like this?"

"I like it. I was born and brought up in Leesfield, and I like it, even so. I suppose you think I should live in New York?"

"Wouldn't it offer you more?"

"You mean all that intellectually stimulating conversation and theater—lights, glamour, excitement?" He laughed. "No thanks. I tried it for a year when I was cramming for the New York bar exam, and I didn't care for it one little bit. That kind of life isn't for me. It's too frantic, you never have any time to be comfortable. Instead I came back here to practice, and after I decided I liked enforcing the law better than trying to get around it, I got elected Chief of Police. Now I'm that and the deputy coroner for this district, and as far as I'm concerned, I can't think of a more satisfactory or rewarding way to spend my time."

"Lucky, lucky," Janice sighed.

"Also, stubborn, and I suppose more than a little lazy." He offered her a cigarette. "What about you?"

"What about me?"

"What's a beautiful doll like you doing here?"

"I've got six weeks of vacation, and Roundmount beckoned."

"You left out the vital statistics," he reminded her. "After all, it's only fair, I gave you a complete history."

"I'm five seven, I have no intention of telling you what I weigh, I'm divorced, and I enjoy excellent health."

"Divorced? Who was so foolish?"

"You're very sweet, as well as stubborn," Janice said. "You don't really want to know, do you?"

"As a matter of fact, I do."

"All right, then, you asked for it. I got married while I was a senior in college to a boy who wanted to write. I believed in his talent, so after we graduated I worked to

93

support us both while he learned his trade. He was talented, he wrote a wonderful book, eventually it got published and made a lot of money, and he was on his way—and the next thing I knew he didn't need a mommy anymore, and I was out of a husband and a marriage."

"Just like that?"

"Just like that."

"Any children?"

"No. That's the one thing I'm grateful for in the whole deal, that we were free to separate without hurting anybody else." She stubbed out her cigarette. "That's enough of that. What about Arlene? Was her death really an accident?"

"Probably not. There's good reason to think it was suicide."

"Ezra said he thought it might be. She was pretty flaky."

"So I've been told, but that's only part of it. Dr. Agnew said yesterday that both of you stopped in at a party that Roger Benton gave after Arlene played."

"Yes."

"How many other people were there?"

"Oh, maybe fifteen or twenty, almost all students. Miranda was there for a while with those visiting Germans, but they left before we did, and Ezra and I left before Cathleen and Horace. We only stayed for about an hour or so. Most of them looked as if they'd be good for all night, but we were too bored to do that. College kids are no longer my idea of stimulating company."

"Was there anything out of the way about Arlene's behavior there?"

"She seemed more alive—oh dear, that's not the best word to use under the circumstances, is it? Well, more animated than when I'd ever seen her before. On the other hand, I didn't know her at all well, since Cathleen and I aren't staying in the dorm, but in those rooms over the dining hall. I thought Ezra gave her a couple of awfully clinical looks, and he asked her if we could walk her home, but she said no, for which you could hardly blame her since she seemed to be having fun. Maybe part of it was that she hadn't unwound from playing."

"Had Benton arranged this party before the concert?"

"My God, no. You must've heard that announcement he made which was truly on the spur of the moment. Nothing is structured around this place, including the social life."

"Do you know Roger well?"

Janice shrugged. "We see each other now and then in the city."

"I'm not inquiring into your personal history. What I'm asking is do you know him well enough to tell me how he'd behave in a certain situation?"

"Like what?"

"Ezra said he thought Roger had his eye on Arlene. Do you think that's right?"

"Of course he did, Roger has his eye on every girl he sees." She bit her lip. "Sorry. I have no right to say that, it's not really my business."

"Was there much drinking?"

"There was plenty of beer at the picnic, and a couple of bottles of hard liquor at Roger's."

"Grass too, I suppose."

"Possibly."

"Was Roger stoned or drunk?"

She sat up straight. "What's this all about?"

"I asked you if he was sober?"

"How can I know that? It's his head."

"Assuming he had his eye on Arlene, and assuming merely for the sake of argument that he was perhaps not entirely in control, do you think he'd try to use—force —on Arlene?''

"Force? Do you mean would he rape her? Is that what happened to her?" She stared at Owen. "I can't believe that Roger would. Or can I?''

Owen decided to be partly frank. "She died by drowning," he said, "and she was conscious when she went into that pothole—water in the lungs and all that. It happened sometime early yesterday morning, and the autopsy also showed that sometime not too long before she died—that is, during the night—she'd been raped. Or at least had had sexual intercourse that involved a physical assault. There's only a couple of things that could've happened. Either somebody at Roundmount raped her, after which she went and drowned herself. Or else she walked into the woods, stripping off her clothes as she went, and someone then either followed her into the woods or came across her there and raped her, after which she drowned herself or was pushed in and drowned. The first seems by far the most plausible possibility, doesn't it?''

"It's hard to believe a man would hang around in the middle of the night on the off chance he'd come across some girl, isn't it?''

"It could happen, though.''

"That poor baby." Janice drew meaningless doodles with some drops of spilled water. "So that she wandered away, like Ophelia.''

" 'Poor Ophelia, divided from herself and her fair judgment'?''

"Yes." She looked up. "Literally scared to death.''

"I'm afraid so.''

"What kind of a miserable man would insist on having his own way with a child like her?''

"Do you think Roger would have?''

96

"He—oh, it's too hideous to think about. But who else was there?"

"I've gone over what happened in such detail," Miranda was saying at the faculty meeting, "because we thought first of all you should know the real truth, and secondly, because to be frank we need help in deciding the best way to handle the situation. As I'm sure you all realize by this time, Arlene, although she was tremendously gifted, was not quite—mentally secure." Several of the people sitting around the room nodded solemnly. "I'm sure her parents hoped that Roundmount's artistically free life and healthy country atmosphere would be helpful to Arlene. But apparently not."

"Apparently," someone echoed sarcastically.

"Did you say something?"

"Just agreeing with you," Dave answered.

"I'm sure you did everything you could for her, Mandy," the viola teacher said loyally, glaring at Dave, who returned the hostile look with interest. Miranda acknowledged the support with a grateful nod.

"Well, I do know that I did nothing to contribute to her death, and neither did anyone else here. I sincerely believe her unfortunate fate was inevitable, and that we have nothing to reproach ourselves for. And however shocking it is, we can't change what's already happened.

"But we do have to deal with its aftermath. Stories and gossip about this event are sure to circulate, not just in the village but all through the Berkshires. Not only that, but some of the younger people here will probably mention it to their parents, which means that we're going to get phone calls from them, too.

"The best way to handle any inquiries, I think, is simply to tell the truth. Nobody can stop someone who

97

truly wants to commit suicide. They always find a way. It was our misfortune that Roundmount looked like a good place to drown herself to Arlene."

"Just a minute," David said. "Do I understand you correctly? You want us to say that *we* are the true victims of that poor crazy kid's act? That if she hadn't been so selfish and inconsiderate she would have picked some other place to kill herself?"

"Dave, let me tell you something. I've already had two calls this morning from reporters in Boston, who found out about this somehow, one of them said from a parent of one of the kids. I am only trying to protect Roundmount and all the rest of you here, too, from that kind of bad publicity. If anyone asks you about it, what I want is for you to make it plain that we had nothing to do with what happened, that's all, that she alone was responsible. You don't have to make a point of saying she was ill, but—"

"For God's sake, Haller," Roger put in, "There's no disgrace involved in being sick. How unenlightened can you be? Besides," he added, "she's dead. She'll never know what you say about her."

"Now, as far as her parents're concerned," Miranda went on hastily, "they're flying here and'll get in early this afternoon. If you have occasion to meet them, naturally I'm sure you'll want to express your sympathy and regret for their loss. But if you talk to them for any length of time, I think it would be an act of mercy if you'd do everything you can to reinforce the idea that Arlene got as much loving attention during her short stay here as we could possibly give her. That way you'll help them feel better, and perhaps lessen their grief a trifle. It's really a great consolation in tragic circumstances like these for a family to be certain that everything possible has been done for the one who's—passed on."

She scanned their faces. "Does anybody have any questions?"

"Will there be a funeral?" Dave asked.

"Certainly not," Miranda said, outraged. "They'll take her body back with them, and she'll be buried at home where she belongs." She got up. "If there's nothing else, meeting's adjourned." Then she raised her voice over the noise of chairs scraping against the floor. "Oh, one more thing. The parents'll probably have dinner with us here in the dining room tonight. Out of respect, would everybody please dress more formally than usual? Skirts for the women, and shirts and ties for the men. Dinner'll be at the usual time. I'll type out some memos about this and post them on the bulletin boards for the students, so they'll know."

Roger came over to her. "Do you need somebody to go to the airport with you to pick them up? If you do, I'll be glad to come along. Then I could drive back."

"Thanks, Roger. That would be so nice of you."

He took her hand and pressed it sympathetically, while Horace watched. When Roger left, he said to Miranda, "That's not such a hot idea, to take Roger with you."

"Why not? I want to pick them up myself so I can talk to them before anyone else does. You can't come with me because one of us has to be around to answer the phone if the papers call again. I don't want to have to drive back myself at the same time I'm trying to deal with them."

"Get somebody else to go with you."

"Why?"

"Because, stupid, Roger wants to go with you so he can make sure nobody so much as mentions he even knew Arlene. What he's trying to do is cover his own ass on your time."

99

Owen was waiting when Miranda got to the office. She listened to what he had to say about the autopsy report, but before he could begin to ask her any questions, she was counterattacking.

"I don't believe it."

"What do you mean, you don't believe it? Do you think Frank Burch made this up?"

"I simply do not believe it," she repeated. "In the first place, that girl was insane, out and out insane. God knows what she was capable of doing, or with whom, or where. In the second place, I can't believe anybody here would be that brutal. I know everyone quite well, and I can assure you—"

"Miranda," Owen said, in a voice of stone, "that girl, insane or not, was beaten and raped. You may not like to admit it, but that's what happened. It's my duty to investigate this crime and to prosecute if the evidence I find warrants it. So don't get any ideas about trying to persuade me to drop it."

"She wasn't raped at Roundmount."

"She didn't leave the grounds at any time during the night. She was here, and you know it."

"Owen, listen. Even if it is true, even if it did happen, what difference does it make?"

"What *difference*?"

"Listen, Owen. She's dead. Suppose she'd stayed in that pothole a little longer and the turtles had finished picking her clean. You'd never've known anything about this at all, because there would have been only bones left. This is no way for me to be treated. All I did was try to help her. If you don't keep this quiet, it'll only destroy the living and it won't make any difference to the dead, it can't. Her parents will suffer, I'll suffer, Roundmount will be ruined, and it's all for nothing. You can't change things, you can't make her alive again. It's not as if she'd come to me and complained about being molested by someone. If she had I would certainly have done something, called you in at once, if only to find out if what she was saying was true or just another one of her crazy fantasies—"

"Now wait a minute!"

"Don't you see, you're not able to help her now, you can't, and you're doing a lot to hurt other people? It's bad enough to have to admit that one of our students committed suicide—do you have any idea what a story about rape would do to Roundmount?"

"I don't care—"

"But I do! And her parents will! Why, you might even kill them with grief. Forget it, Owen! It's the only way!"

"I certainly will not and cannot forget it. It's my job, I have a responsibility—"

"You're being vindictive, that's all."

"Vindictive? Toward whom?"

"To me—Horace—her parents."

"For Christ's sake, why would I—"

"I don't know why. As far as I knew, we've always been good friends."

"Miranda," Owen made one last attempt. "There's such a thing as the law, as justice."

"Justice? For whom, may I ask? Even if she were assaulted, which I don't admit, how can you say that the man was the one responsible for it, especially now that she's dead? I know what girls are like, I've seen them in action a thousand times. They get into impossible situations with men so innocently, and then after they've asked for it they decide to change their minds. And when they find out it's too late, then they yell rape. Who's to blame, I ask you? Them or the men? And what justice is there in making one of them the goat and not the other?"

"So much for women's lib! For the first time I truly

understand what they mean when they talk about blaming the victim. Let me remind you, this girl didn't complain about anybody or anything. All she did was kill herself over it, that's all! But I can see this is impossible, there's no point in even talking to you." He stalked out in such a fury that he didn't even know he was outside till he found himself on the lawn. Too angry to have a clear idea of what he ought to do next, he walked rapidly up the road till he reached Roger's cabin. He knocked and peered in; Roger wasn't home. Still fuming he walked back down the hill, avoiding the main house by cutting through the field instead of coming down the road. He passed the music barn; through its window there floated the reedy sounds of a small chamber orchestra rehearsing something by, he guessed, Haydn. They broke off just as he came level with the door, and he looked in. A dozen or so instrumentalists were sitting there; a boy who couldn't have been more than twenty was conducting, perched on a high wooden stool in front of the equally young or younger players. Owen recognized him as one of the students he'd talked to, a very bright southern boy. He was saying now, in a voice that perfectly expressed long-suffering patience, "All raht, Burton, what's yo' count, fo' or eight?"

"Eight," one of the doublebass players replied sheepishly, moving the tip of his bow along the music before him.

"Then come in on one, not five, okay?"

"Okay."

The conductor extended his arms; holding the baton in his right hand as grandly as if he were commanding the attention of an entire philharmonic, he hit the tip end against the side of his outstretched left forefinger. "Heah we go," he said, happily encouraging. "From C. One, two—come in, violins," and they began again.

Owen listened for a few minutes; they were as awful as only young players can be, but they were all so obviously delighted with themselves and with the music that their pleasure was contagious, and he moved away down the hill a little calmer.

He found Ezra and Dave in the art shed, and asked if they'd seen Roger.

"He's teaching now," Dave replied. "He'll be out at half-past."

"Where's his class?"

"In one of the buildings or out in the field, I don't know," Dave said. "The way he teaches it doesn't make any difference where he is. The best thing to do is to go to the dining hall at lunchtime, you'll be sure to find him there."

"Will I be in the way if I wait here?"

"No, we weren't working," Ezra said. "We were gossiping about Arlene just like everybody else. Dave's been telling me about the faculty meeting they've just had. Apparently Miranda intends to sweep the whole thing under the rug as soon as possible. I'll bet by the middle of next month if someone mentions Arlene Horowitz to her, she won't even recognize the name."

"You can't entirely blame her," Dave said. "After all, she has a big stake in Roundmount, and if there's too much talk about this, it'll ruin everything she's worked for all these years. You know how it goes. Somebody mentions Roundmount, and somebody else says, Oh, yes, that's the place where a girl got killed, what was it? she drowned. And it may be all they say, but it's enough to put a lot of people off for good."

"When you talked to Arlene," Owen asked Ezra, "did you get the impression she might've killed herself this summer even if she—"

"Even if what?"

"Even if she hadn't been here?"

103

Ezra shook his head. "How many times do I have to tell you I can't give you an opinion on a half-hour's worth of conversation that wasn't intended to be a consultation? I'd have to know much more about her history, and even then the best I could do would be an informed guess. Why not ask her doctor?"

"If I find out who he was, and get a report from the hospital, do you think you could tell me then?"

"Is it so important that you have an answer?"

"It's necessary."

"Okay, I'll try. But I warn you, you'll never know for sure. You can't."

"I'll have a better idea than I do now."

"Perhaps." His reply was almost drowned in a great metallic clanging. Across the field a stout woman dressed in a white uniform was beating a rusty iron triangle with a cooking fork.

"That's lunch." Dave got up. "Come on."

"What's your hurry?" Ezra asked. "It's not going to be worth running for."

"Isn't the food any good?" Owen asked.

"It's not that it's bad, so much as it is there's never enough. Plain living and high thinking apparently lead to skimpy eating."

"It didn't used to be this bad."

"I've developed a passion for peanut butter and jelly I didn't know I was capable of," Ezra said as the three of them headed for the dining hall. "Most of my dreams seem to revolve around corned beef sandwiches on rye with mustard. How's that for wish fulfillment?"

"It's Horace," Dave said. "Since he's been up here the whole place has been going to hell."

"Watch it," Ezra commented. "You're beginning to sound paranoid. You blame Horace for everything."

"No, I don't. Just for what I don't like."

"There's Roger," Owen said. "I'll see you later." He

cut across the grass. Roger was walking through the field with his head bent attentively toward a student who was talking and looking up with worshipful eyes. Owen overtook them at the foot of the stairs.

"Benton," he said.

Roger turned around. "Oh yes, our yokel Sherlock."

"Will you excuse us, miss?"

The girl looked at their faces and replied faintly, "Yes, sure, of course," and fled up the stairs.

"You'll have to come with me," Owen said.

"Where?"

"To the station for questioning."

"Before lunch? Why can't we talk here?"

"I don't find it convenient."

"Are you arresting me? For what? Where's your warrant?"

"I don't have to arrest you to take you in for questioning. You'll get a chance to call a lawyer if it's necessary."

"Are you kidding? Where would I find a decent lawyer in this hick town?"

"That's your problem, not mine. Are you coming quietly, or shall I use handcuffs?"

Roger measured him up and down, and Owen smiled. "Try," he urged softly. "Do me a favor—try."

"Oh no." Roger shook his head. "You'll have to play country cossack with some other patsy, friend. I'll come, but under protest. And God help you if there's anything the least bit illegal in what you're doing."

"Why, what'll you do? report me to the *New York Post*?"

"Among other things," Roger said, "yes."

Owen stood over Roger until he got into the car. As he was walking around to the driver's seat, a screen door slammed and Miranda came storming out across the lawn.

"Where are you taking him?"

"Down for questioning."

Roger put his head out of the car window. "Sic him, Mandy," he shouted. "I'm being kidnapped."

Miranda managed to control her voice. "Owen, couldn't we—"

"No."

"Where're they going?" Horace asked. He'd come out of the house just in time to return Roger's jaunty wave, and stood beside Miranda watching the car drive down the hill.

"That Owen Henderson's impossible," Miranda said between clenched teeth.

"Are you saying Roger's mixed up in Arlene's death?"

"Owen has some crazy idea she was assaulted."

"Assaulted? How?"

"If you must know, raped."

"By that sonofabitch?"

"No. I don't know. Maybe."

"Whaddeya mean, maybe?"

"It can't be true. It isn't true. Roger promised me he wouldn't go near that adolescent lunatic."

"And you believed him?"

"Of course. Why shouldn't I?"

"For a lot of reasons, all of which you're too stubborn to—"

"Oh, leave me alone."

"I told you more than once get rid of him, but no, you never want to take anybody's advice. And now look."

"Let's not quarrel. I've got to concentrate. How am I going to keep Owen from telling her parents about this idiotic theory?"

"Yes, I'd do that if I were you. And just in case you're not able to keep Owen from telling them, I'd call a good lawyer. It's possible you're about to be sued for everything you've got. Including Roundmount."

11

"Anybody home?" Martin closed the screen behind him and walked into the kitchen.

"Just me. Come on in." Horace was in the living room.

"Thanks." Martin sat down. "Is there anything I can do?" he asked.

"About what?"

"About Arlene's—death."

"You've heard? Thanks. Maybe later, but right now everything's more or less under control. Mandy's gone to the airport to pick up the father and mother. They oughta be back in an hour or so."

"What a terrible shock it must've been for them."

"They're due for a lot bigger one."

Martin waited for Horace to explain, but all he said was, "How about a drink?"

"In the middle of the day?"

"Why not?" He got up and went over to the liquor. "Bourbon okay?"

"Why not?"

As Horace dropped ice cubes into two glasses he said over his shoulder, "You don't like Roger much, do you?"

"Can you think of any reason why I should? He's a rude, insulting, egotistical boor. And what's worse, he's dirty, physically dirty. His shirts look as though he wears them a week. He probably grew that beard so he wouldn't have to wash his face."

"You're right," Horace agreed, "he's not too attractive, is he? At least not to us." He leaned forward and raised his glass. "Let me propose a toast. To Roger's early downfall."

"Well, I wouldn't go so far as to wish him harm," Martin said uneasily.

Horace hooted with laughter. "What the hell good is hating him unless you have the courage of your convictions? Go ahead, Martin, drink to it!"

"Oh, all right." Martin only meant to take a tiny sip to please Horace, but before he put his glass down it was half-empty, and the liquor was a big warm spot in the middle of his stomach.

Horace took a small sip. "You know," he said confidentially, "you and me, in a way we're better off than Roger."

"I should hope so. I wouldn't be like him for anything in the world."

"You don't understand what I'm trying to tell you. People like Roger, they think they've got some kind of charmed life, so they can get away with murder. Well, let me tell you, this time he's gone too far. And he's really in deep trouble."

"You're not making much sense, Horace."

"He's gonna get what's coming to him this time, I feel it in my bones. Because if he doesn't, there's no justice in the world, none at all."

"What are you talking about?"

"You don't know, do you?" He leaned forward and gripped Martin's knee. "Okay, I'll tell you. But you have to promise you won't say anything to Mandy about it, because if she finds out I've told anybody, even you, she'll skin me alive." He slumped back. "You don't know what it's like to be married to a woman like her, you just don't know. She's a bully. But she makes everybody think it's my fault. She has to have an albatross to wear around her neck so the whole world can see what a noble suffering little woman she is. Sometimes I feel like I'm a goddam fur piece.''

"That's not fair to Mandy."

"Never mind Mandy. Let's get back to Roger. Owen's taken him in for questioning.''

"What for?"

"For raping Arlene."

"When?"

"Last night."

"Is that why she—"

"Looks that way. It kinda reminds me of that old joke about the little hen being chased by a rooster who scoots out of the yard and gets run over on the road, and one old maid watching on the porch says to the other old maid, 'Isn't that sweet? She'd rather die!'"

"Stop talking like that, do you hear me! Shut up! Don't you dare make jokes about her, it's not the least bit funny. She's dead. And he killed her, just the same as if he'd put a gun to her head. I hope they—"

"So do I, so do I. But supposing they don't, Martin, supposing they don't. What then?"

"And what happened then?"

"What do you mean, what happened then?" Roger twisted in his chair and scowled up at Owen. "Everybody who wanted to came up to the cabin and we sat around and talked like civilized adults. That's what a party usually is, isn't it?"

"What'd you talk about?"

"The usual things. Literature, music, art—the important things of life, my dear man."

"How many people were there?"

"How should I know? I didn't charge admission, there wasn't any reason to count the house."

"Name some."

"Mandy and Horace, and that art historian and his wife."

"Any other faculty?"

"Cathleen."

"So almost everybody else there was a student, is that right?"

"I guess so."

"When did this scintillating adult group break up?"

"How should I know?"

"Before ten?"

"No."

"Before eleven."

"I doubt it."

"Before twelve?"

"Will you try now for thirteen?"

"Before twelve?"

"Probably not."

"After midnight, then?"

"Look, lover—"

"Are you making as pass at me, sonny?"

"Why, you—"

"I merely like to keep the record straight, that's all. You're in enough trouble as it is without being unjustly accused of homosexual solicitation and attempted sodomy."

Roger drew a very deep breath and folded his arms. "I see I underestimate you."

"Well, we're finally getting someplace," Owen said genially. "Now you've recognized my superiority, it should be easy."

"Your *what*?"

"Who were the last students to leave?"

"I don't remember."

"Did Arlene Horowitz leave with anybody else?"

"I don't remember."

"So she stayed on after everybody else left, was that it?"

110

"I didn't say that."

"Well, who did she leave with, then?"

"I told you, I don't remember."

"Why? Were you so drunk?"

"I wasn't drunk."

"Stoned on grass, then?"

"What grass?"

"If you weren't stoned or drunk, then why can't you remember saying goodnight to your guests?"

"I wasn't drunk and I wasn't stoned and I do remember," Roger shouted.

"Then who did she leave with?"

"With *whom*, you illiterate provincial!"

"Several students who were at this party told me that she didn't leave at all, that she stayed there with you."

Roger had no comment.

Owen opened his notebook. "When the last people were leaving, isn't it true that when Arlene started to go with them, you put your arm around her shoulder and said"—he consulted his notebook—" 'Not just yet, baby, I'll take you home later myself'." He looked at Roger. "Isn't that true?"

"You certainly don't read dialogue very well, I must say," Roger commented critically.

"Possibly because the quality of the lines I have to read is so poor," Owen retorted. "Now, is that true?"

"Is what true?"

"That you prevented Arlene from going home with the others, and that they had no choice but to leave her alone with you in that cabin?"

Roger said, "What the hell is this all about, anyway?"

"I take it then that you wouldn't say the people who reported this conversation to me were lying?"

"I'm not going to say another goddam word until I find out what this is all about." He closed his lips firmly, and then opened them again. "Except for one thing," he said plaintively. "I'm *hungry*. When am I going to get my lunch?"

12

Miranda and Cathleen were the only people waiting at the airfield, which wasn't surprising, since its total plant consisted of a single small hangar, a T-shaped asphalt-paved airstrip, and a limp red windsock. Cathleen surveyed it disdainfully, and said, "Pretty seedy. It's no better than a small town bus station that's in a drug-store."

"What did you expect to find out here," Miranda asked, "Logan Airport? It's only used by small private planes." She pointed. "That must be their plane coming in now."

The monoplane skimmed down onto the landing strip, braked, and taxied bumpily toward them, stopping about fifteen feet from the hangar door. The employee of the airport slouched out of his office and waved to the pilot, who waved back. Miranda got out of the car and walked toward the plane, her head up and her shoulders stiff. Cathleen, left behind, rolled down the window as far as it would go, and leaned her head out, intent on not missing a thing.

The plane door swung open and the young pilot flipped steps out of the cabin, then jumped down them on to the asphalt. A middle-aged man followed right behind him, moving almost as athletically. His dark suit hung on his spare stooped frame; he had iron-gray hair cropped short, an unattractive raw-skinned, thin-lipped face, and an air of authoritative assurance. He and the pilot walked away from the steps and conferred for a few minutes. Mr. Horowitz did most of the talking, gesturing abruptly now and then with a skinny hand, while the pilot listened respectfully and nodded his head. As they talked a tall, pimply-faced youngster—Cathleen thought, he must be the son, and he's going to look just like his father, poor boy—poked his head out of the cabin, said something to somebody inside, then carried two small suitcases down the steps and put them on the asphalt. He went back up the steps and held his hand out; a stout woman, dressed entirely in black, made an appearance, and the boy very carefully and solicitously supported her down the steps and away from the plane.

Miranda walked up to them and said something, Cathleen couldn't hear what. The woman stared at her, then averted her head, took a handkerchief out of her black pocketbook, and held it so it covered most of her broad, olive-skinned face. The son, obviously embarrassed, said nothing. The man came over, and greeted Miranda with a curt nod and a word or two. He paid no attention to his wife's tears. The boy picked up one suitcase and his father the other; then the four of them proceeded to the car, Mrs. Horowitz leaning heavily on her son's arm, her face still buried in her handkerchief, Mr. Horowitz and Miranda pacing a bit faster in front of them.

"Yes," he was saying to her as they came to the car, "I've decided it would pay for me to get my own plane. It's getting to be too expensive to do anything else. Why, this month alone it's cost me—"

"Why don't you and Mrs. Horowitz ride in back with me?" Miranda broke in, "and your son—Bernard, isn't it?—can get in front with Miss Linton."

Mrs. Horowitz reluctantly let Bernard help her into the car, and once in, shifted her body painfully crabwise and planted herself solidly in the middle of the back seat. "Oh," Miranda said. "I'll go around, then." She let herself in the other door, while Mr. Horowitz fitted himself into the vacant place at his wife's right.

Bernard put the luggage in the trunk, then got into the front seat and nodded to Cathleen. Without a word he took a book out of his pocket, opened it, and at once began to read. Cathleen was greatly relieved. She'd been afraid that he'd want to talk to her and she wouldn't be able to listen to everything that was said in the back seat. She drove off, very successfully giving the impression that she was completely oblivious to her passengers. She did glance over at Bernard now and then, though, and eventually she saw that his apparent disinterest in the conversation was as false as her own, and that actually he was eavesdropping too. Aware of her eyes on him, he looked up. They exchanged a brief conspiratorial glance, and after that, although he still kept his head studiously bent, he didn't bother to turn the pages any more except once in a while.

For the first few miles there was no sound except Mrs. Horowitz's heavy bursts of sighing. Then her husband, as Cathleen had decided he might, began an attack by saying peremptorily, "Now, Mrs. Boardman, suppose you tell me exactly what happened. Where did you go wrong?"

"I did tell you what happened on the phone." Both of them had to lean forward to talk across Mrs. Horowitz, who didn't move her head either left or right.

"Everything?"

"You can tell me why," Mrs. Horowitz wailed, still looking straight ahead, "why you didn't watch over her carefully."

"My dear Mrs. Horowitz," Miranda interrupted, "Roundmount is not a day care center. We don't watch over anybody here. I did nothing wrong. I made no promises to you of any kind, please remember that, and furthermore, I disclaim all responsibility for what happened. It is your own fault entirely that you never told me anything about the nature and extent 'of Arlene's illness, for if you had I would certainly have told you that you should send her somewhere else for the summer."

"If you didn't mean to take care of her, then why did you bring her up here?" Mrs. Horowitz burst out in a kind of screaming sob that startled Cathleen so much she swerved into the oncoming lane.

"Riba, keep quiet," her husband commanded.

"My baby lies dead, and you don't want me to complain? My Arlene, my genius girl, lies drowned, and it's too much for you if I should cry, if I should ask why should it have happened? Is that the kind of feeling you have for your only daughter?" She began to sob loudly into her handkerchief, and Bernard shifted uneasily, but didn't look around. Mr. Horowitz made an angry wordless sound, sat back, and looked out the window, absolutely refusing to acknowledge her display of grief. Miranda gazed at the heaving black-clad bulk next to her, lifted her hand toward it as if to offer comfort, then shook her head, perplexed, and sat back herself. The second the sobbing began to abate, Mr. Horowitz bent forward again.

"Who's taking care of the body?"

"Why, I believe—" Miranda, busy with her own thoughts, had been taken by surprise—"that it's at the undertaker's. Dr. Burch arranged for it, I think."

"What do you mean, you believe, you think? Don't you know?"

"The body," Miranda said firmly, "is at the funeral home in Leesfield."

"Is this Dr. Burch attached to the school?"

"No, he's the—"

"You mean there's no doctor at the camp?"

"Yes, there's a doctor there, but—"

"What's his name?"

"Agnew."

"Agnew? Never heard of him. Where's he practice?"

"New York. He's a psychiatrist."

"Psychiatrist, eh? Was he treating Arlene?"

Mrs. Horowitz blew her nose and re-entered the conversation. "Who's this local horse doctor? When did you call him in?"

"I didn't. He's the medical examiner, the police called him in."

"Medical examiner? Police? What's a medical examiner? What's he got to do with my baby?" For the first time Mrs. Horowitz turned her head to look at Miranda directly, her red-rimmed eyes suspicious.

"The law in Connecticut is—that is, the medical examiner has to—has to be called in when—in any case of—when somebody dies from—" Miranda took a deep breath and began again. "In Connecticut the medical examiner has to certify any case of violen—when a person doesn't die from a natural illness."

"You mean—oh, Milton," she turned to her husband, instantly hysterical again, "does that mean they're going to cut her up all over and look at her insides? Milton, don't let them! You know how I feel about that, you know I can't bear when somebody isn't all together. Don't let them touch her. She's got to be whole when she's buried, all whole, or I don't know what I'll do."

Miranda closed her eyes.

Cathleen thought, Dear God, she didn't tell them about the turtles, and stepped on the gas.

"Riba, will you keep quiet, I can hardly hear myself think!"

"They're cutting her up into little pieces right this

116

minute, I know they are!"

"No, they aren't, don't be foolish. Now stop! How do you expect I can find out anything if you keep interrupting?"

"Look," Miranda said desperately over the noise of Mrs. Horowitz's keening, "we're almost there, and since we don't seem to be able to talk now, why don't we wait until you've rested up a little from your trip, and then we can sit down and get everything arranged in a civilized manner?"

"Very well," Mr. Horowitz agreed. Then he added, with a certain amount of sardonic relish, "but in case you don't already know it, Mrs. Boardman, I'll tell you something. My wife isn't a very civilized woman, and in matters that are important to me, I'm a man not easily satisfied with anybody else's ideas about arrangements."

Horace was waiting when they got to the house, calm and properly subdued. He took charge of Mrs. Horowitz in a professional way that she recognized at once as permission to be emotional. She immediately responded by sinking into another crying fit. Horace and Bernard between them managed to get her to her room. Once there, Bernard took a bottle out of the suitcase, and coaxed her into taking two capsules and lying down. In the meantime Miranda showed Mr. Horowitz to his room and left him to wash up, promising to talk to him as soon as he'd rested; then she went downstairs and took her own tranquilizer, a quick stiff shot of bourbon.

The minute Horace appeared Miranda asked, "Has Henderson called? Where's Roger?"

"Not a word from either of them. What happened on the drive home?"

"Nothing. I couldn't talk to them at all. She was

117

making too much noise. Horace, I've got to speak to Owen."

"Call him."

"I can't, they'll hear. I'll have to go down there."

"They'll see you leave."

"Not if I go out the back door. The car's in the side driveway." She looked at her watch. "I'll try to get back as soon as I can. If he comes down before I do, stall him. Tell him something important came up and I had to go out for a minute."

"All right."

"Did you speak to Lester?"

He nodded. "That's good," and she was gone, closing the back door quietly behind her. From the upstairs hall window Bernard watched her dodge across the lawn, keeping close to the bushes around the house.

Owen was in the outer office at the police station. Without preamble, she said, "I've got to talk to you, Owen."

"What about?"

"Arlene's parents are here. What am I to tell them?"

"Not a thing. I'll talk to them myself."

"Owen, I wish you'd realize—" Miranda caught herself. "Very well," she said. "Shall I bring them down here, or will you come up?"

"Suit yourself."

"I'll bring them—or him, by himself, if I can manage it—down here, then. He'll have to go to the undertaker's, anyway." She paused. "Look, Owen, they're terribly difficult people. The mother's already had hysterics three times."

"That's hardly surprising, considering the circumstances."

"Oh, yes, I know that sounds unfeeling," Miranda retorted. "However, I suggest you meet them before you presume to judge me. Believe me, they don't make

118

it easy to feel sorry for them. I shudder to think what's going to happen when she sees the body. Owen, I want to ask a favor of you."

"Now what?"

"Please—will you please not say anything to them right away about this theory that she was assaulted?"

"Mir—"

"No, wait till I've finished. I'm not asking you to drop the investigation or anything like that, and I can see that I was foolish to've done it this morning, but you'll have to forgive me, I was a little hysterical myself. But you surely don't have enough proof against anybody yet to arrest them or anything like that, do you?"

He hestitated, then shook his head.

"Well, wouldn't it be possible not to tell them about it until you have? Or if you won't do that, couldn't you at least—please, Owen—put off telling them till tomorrow, so I won't have them on my hands overnight while they're brooding about it?"

"I can't promise you anything."

"There's another thing, you know. I can't be responsible for what might happen to Mrs. Horowitz if you do insist on telling her. She's got a weak heart, and she's close to collapse as it is."

"No one's asking you to be responsible."

She sighed. "Very well. But honestly, I can't see what difference it'll make to you or to them if they find out tonight or tomorrow, except that it gives Horace and me a lot more trouble."

"That's too bad. Sometimes trouble can't be helped."

Miranda looked him in the eye. "I never thought of you as being so self-righteous."

Owen colored. "I'm not—I'll have to see the situation for myself," he finished lamely. But it was obvious

119

that that was as much of a concession as he was going to make.

"All right," Miranda said, "if that's what you insist on." She started to walk out, then after a few steps turned back. "By the way," she said, "I don't suppose you went over to the stables to talk to Lester, did you?"

"Lester? You mean Les Grant? No, why?"

"You know, Arlene rode a lot—she had her own horse here, and Les told Horace that on the day she died she'd come back in and said that she'd been thrown. So that's probably what her bruises were from."

"Is that so? Did Les just come around and volunteer this information?"

"Well—they happened to be talking about her, and Les remembered this and mentioned it during the conversation, that's all."

"I see." Owen frowned thoughtfully at the end of his pencil. "Miranda, I bet you have the idea that an assault by force is necessary for the charge of rape."

"I don't understand."

"In this state," he said, his voice harsh, "rape is also defined as a sexual act committed with a girl or woman who is of unsound mind. Even if the girl consents to the act, if the man doesn't have to use any force at all, it's still rape if she doesn't have the use of all her mental faculties, if she isn't able to judge rationally what she's doing."

"Oh, really? I didn't know that," Miranda said in a small voice. "That *is* interesting."

"Now, this morning you told me that Arlene Horowitz was insane—'out and out insane' was the phrase you used, wasn't it?"

Miranda made a helpless gesture and started to leave.

"Wait just one minute," Owen said.

She looked around.

"You can take Benton back with you, I'm through

with him temporarily."

"Where is he?"

"He yelled about being hungry, so I sent him out with Mike to have lunch. They ought to be back any minute."

"All right. I'll wait for them in the car. It's right outside." They showed up before she was halfway through her cigarette. Roger waved to her as Mike escorted him into the station. He emerged in a few minutes, smiling, and came around to her window. "Move over," he ordered, "I'll drive."

"No you won't," Miranda replied. "Come on, hurry up and get in."

He went around to the other door. "How'd you work that?" he asked.

"Work what?"

"Getting me out of the Gestapo's clutches."

"I didn't do anything, Owen told me to wait for you because he was through for now."

"Huh." He didn't say anything for a few minutes, then he asked, "What's this all about, anyway? I still don't know why he wanted to question me, he wouldn't tell me."

"You're sure you don't know?" Miranda asked sarcastically. "Just as innocent as a little lamb, are you?"

"Cross my heart," Roger answered promptly. "I don't know what the hell I'm supposed to've done."

"Roger, I told you to keep your hands off that girl!!"

"Now see here, sugar, I just put in a tough couple of hours with him, I don't have to take any crap from you on top of it."

"*You've* put in a tough couple of hours, well, that's too bad. So have I and so has Horace. And it's not over yet. You've got a nerve to complain to me."

"Who's complaining? I can take care of myself. All I want to know is what's going on."

"Is there any reason why you couldn't leave her alone? She wasn't that attractive, there're lots of other—"

"Who, for instance? You? Miranda, let me remind you that we agreed we wouldn't make any demands on each—"

"Demands? All I'm asking is that you don't rape the students and drive them to suicide. I don't think, Roger, that that's being excessively deman—"

"Rape? Is *that* what this's all about? Ridiculous!"

"Did you?"

"Did I what?"

"Did you rape her?"

"Certainly not! For Christ's sake, I've never had to rape a girl in my whole life. You ought to know."

"Did you—"

"What now, doll?"

"Did you—" The words stuck in her throat, and he made the mistake of laughing. "You know, Mandy, I think you'd be happier if I didn't answer that question. What do you think?"

Goaded beyond endurance, Miranda replied savagely, "I think you can start packing as soon as we get back to Roundmount, Roger. You're through."

"*What*?"

"You heard me. There's been enough scandal here for one summer. I can't take any more chances with what else you might do."

"Like hell!"

"I mean it!"

"Well, you damn well better reconsider," he shouted back. "You can't afford to fire me!"

"What do you mean, I can't afford—"

"If you think you're going to make me the scapegoat for this mess, you'd better think again, that's all! If you make me leave, I'll write to the parents of every single kid here, giving them my side of the story, and including all the lurid details of life at Roundmount while I'm doing it. What I don't know and haven't seen, I'll make up. And that'd be just the begin—''

"Are you trying to blackmail me, you bastard?"

"Just don't make the mistake of thinking I wouldn't try to defend myself, that's all. And for another thing, what about my contract? I'll sue you for—''

"You'll get paid, don't worry. Whatever it costs to get you off the premises'll be worth it."

"But I'm not going," he said, suddenly very reasonable and self-possessed. "It's too good a deal for me, I'll be damned if I'll give it up."

Miranda slammed the car to a halt in front of the house. "At this point," she said, "I fervently hope that Owen not only can and does prove you raped her, but that he manages to get you twenty years in jail for doing it."

"You'd better hope again, sweetheart. The publicity of a trial like that wouldn't do Roundmount any good, would it? Particularly when I'm so goddam indiscreet."

They both banged the doors getting out.

"We'll talk about this later!" Miranda stalked past him toward the house. She had her foot on the doorstep when Mr. Horowitz said from the hallway, "Well, it's about time, Mrs. Boardman, I've been waiting for you for almost an hour."

"I am terribly sorry," Miranda replied with not the slightest tinge of regret in her voice. "Mr. Horowitz, can you come down to the village with me right away? There's something I must discuss with you, and Mr. Henderson, the deputy coroner for this district, would also like to talk to you."

"Certainly." He came out and they started across the lawn.

"Milton," a plaintive voice called from an upstairs

window, "Milton, where are you going?"

He paid no attention. It was Miranda who looked up to say, "We'll be back in a minute, Mrs. Horowitz."

"Lie down, Riba," Mr. Horowitz commanded over his shoulder, and marched past Roger as if he were invisible.

"Milton—" The appeal hung in the late afternoon air, tearladen, despairing, insistent, and denied.

13

No sooner were they on their way than Miranda, still buoyed by the momentum of her quarrel with Roger, plunged recklessly at her disagreeable task. "Mr. Horowitz," she announced, "I have a confession to make. I haven't been entirely frank with you."

"Aha," he said in a satisfied voice. "I knew it. I could tell there's something you've been trying to hide from me."

"Indeed? You'll see why in a moment, and you may thank me for it, too," Miranda retorted. "The place where we found Arlene's body isn't too far from here— right off this road, as a matter of fact." She gestured. "There's a brook in there that runs through the woods. It's pretty shallow except for one particularly deep spot, which is where she—"

"Drowned herself," he supplied. "I don't like to mince words, Mrs. Boardman."

"Very well, drowned herself. It so happens that there're a number of snapping turtles that live in and around the stream, and unfortunately, Mr. Horowitz" —her voice faltered—"they—they found your

124

daughter's body before we did."

"Turtles?" Mr. Horowitz was puzzled. "Found her? I don't understand."

"Snapping turtles," Miranda explained, her mouth dry, "are scavengers. They eat anything, alive or—dead."

"You mean—they ate Arlene?"

She nodded, without looking at him. "Oh—" he breathed a sound of pure pain. "My daughter—they ate my daughter!" He turned his head away, and Miranda concentrated on maneuvering the car around the worst curve on the hill and out onto the valley road. After a few minutes she said, "I'm sorry I had to tell you this terrible thing. You'll probably want to tell your wife yourself, I suppose."

"Riba? I can't tell her any such story," Mr. Horowitz said heavily. "I don't dare. I'd never hear the end of it. I know," he said, his spirits reviving a trifle as he rose to the challenge of intrigue, "I'll tell her I sent the body on ahead, right away. Once we're home I can manage to keep her from seeing it, that won't be too hard."

"Will she believe you?"

"Of course she will. I usually get things done in a hurry."

"And Bernard?"

"Bernard? What's he got to do with this? He's got nothing to say about it."

"Here we are." Miranda parked in front of the funeral home. "Do you want me to come in with you?"

He refused her offer of support with some dignity, and walked up to the door with his usual quick stride. He was out again in less than ten minutes. From a distance he looked still very much in command of himself; when he got closer, though, Miranda saw that his hands were trembling, and his face was blotchy and wet from crying. She gave him a few minutes to settle himself, then asked sympathetically, "Do you feel up to talking to Henderson now or would you rather go back?"

"Feel up to it? Of course I feel up to it," he replied brusquely. "Let's go."

Owen wasn't at the station. Mike said he'd gone home, but he'd left word that if they came in, they should go over there, he was expecting them. Owen's mother opened the door for them, led them into the den, and said that Owen'd be right down, he was taking a shower.

Mr. Horowitz looked around the large, cheerfully comfortable room, and sank wearily into one of the chairs. "You certainly have an informal way of doing police business up here," he remarked.

Owen came in, and Miranda introduced them. "Miranda," Owen said, "if you don't mind, you'll have to excuse us. You could go into the kitchen. My mother's just put up a fresh pot of coffee."

"No thanks."

"Or if you don't want to wait, I'll be glad to drive Mr. Horowitz up when we're through."

She considered. "Well, if you—" She turned to Mr. Horowitz. "Would you mind very much if I did leave? There's a million things I have to take care of."

"Sure, go ahead, just as long as I get back I don't care who takes me." He waved her away. "But remember," he called after her, "don't say anything to my wife, let me handle it."

"Yes, of course, don't worry." Owen closed the door after her, and she lingered in the hall for a minute, ostensibly to comb her hair in front of the hall mirror. She heard Owen say, "I do regret having to question you, Mr. Horowitz, at a time like this when I know you're so troubled, but I—"

"No need to spend time apologizing. The quicker you get to the point, the less troubled I'll be."

"Er—yes," Owen replied, obviously taken aback. Somewhat cheered by this beginning, Miranda left, smiling a little at what she suspected was in store for Owen.

"Why do you have to see me, anyway?"

"As deputy coroner for this district I have to make a report for all deaths that aren't due to natural illness."

"What has to go in the report?"

"I've already gotten most of the information from Mrs. Boardman, but I'll check some of it with you, if I may. Arlene was nineteen?"

"That's right."

"She was born in Chicago?"

"No, Cleveland. We moved later to Chicago, but Cleveland's where she was born."

"Has she ever made any other attempts at—"

"Suicide, Mr. Henderson? Really, I cannot understand why you people feel so delicate about these words. Doesn't anybody ever die up here?"

"Suicide?"

"No."

"I understand from Mrs. Boardman that she had a history of mental illness."

"Mrs. Boardman," Arlene's father snapped, "is a busybody and a gossip. It's not true. She was *not* crazy."

"Then she wasn't hospitalized?"

"Foolishness, expensive foolishness, that's all that was. She didn't want to give a concert, she pretended to have a breakdown, and my wife fell for it. If I hadn't been out of town she'd never've gotten away with it. But the minute my back is turned, the two of them do what they want. I know it. They don't kid me. They think they do, but they don't. They didn't even tell me she was in that place until I got back, but when I did, she came home in a hurry, let me tell you."

127

Owen stared at him. "But what did the doctors—"

"Doctors! Hah! Do you know one doctor who's ever willing to say somebody's healthy? *I* don't. Why should I believe them? I could see for myself there was nothing wrong with her. She was a perfectly healthy normal girl. Anybody could see that. Nothing wrong with her at all." He crossed his legs and swung the top one back and forth angrily. "You listen to the doctors, you'll spend your whole life being sick," he went on. "They weren't even helping her anyway. And if you want to know what was wrong with her, I'll tell you—she was doing it out of spite."

Owen started to ask what "it" was, but never got a chance, for Mr. Horowitz was rushing on. "And she knew what she was doing all the time. She was running out on me, and she knew it, and I knew it. I was a poor boy, Mr. Henderson. I didn't get where I am today all by my own efforts by letting people put things over on me. Let me assure you, nobody—nobody—runs out on Milton Horowitz."

"Mr. Horowitz, I—"

"Why should I have stood for it?" he demanded, his face contorted with anger. "No reason at all. Just because she's my daughter, she thinks she's going to be able to cheat me. Well, she's wrong, wrong!" He rubbed his hand over his forehead. "Sorry. I didn't mean to yell like that, I'm a little upset, sorry."

Owen was frozen silent.

"And let me tell you another thing," Mr. Horowitz said, again in a frenzy. "This suicide, it's nothing but spite too, that's all it is. Once she saw she couldn't get away with that make-believe business about being crazy, once she knew she was going to have to pay up—"

"Pay up?"

"Certainly, pay up. What do you think? All that money for pianos, music lessons, concerts, trips, special

128

tutors, God knows what else—thousands of dollars, thousands! Not that I wasn't glad to do it," he added immediately, "and I was only doing it for her sake, it was all for her sake, so she could be a concert artist. And after I spent all that money, all of a sudden she's going to decide it's no good. Just a kid, what does she know? And I'm supposed to forget it. Why shouldn't she pay up?"

"But how? What was she supposed to do?"

"How? By keeping her end of the bargain, that's how, by making me, Milton Horowitz, proud of her, so everybody could see, so I'd have something to show off for all those years. And instead of that—" He stopped, then burst out resentfully, "She was always a willful child. It's all Riba's fault, she would never listen to me. She always takes her side. She *always* gets between us."

When Owen thought he could trust his voice again, he asked, "Who was her doctor?"

"Doctor—oh, you mean there? I don't know, I don't remember what his name was."

"What hospital was she in?"

"I couldn't tell you that either," Mr. Horowitz said indifferently. "I forget the name."

"Well, who's your family doctor?"

"Don't have one."

Owen shut his notebook so violently that he dropped it. Bending to pick it up, he said, "I think that about covers everything I have to say to you, Mr. Horowitz. If you're ready, I'll take you up to Roundmount."

They had nothing further to say to each other, except that once, after they'd slewed around one of the curves on the hill because Owen was driving too fast, Mr. Horowitz commented, "This sure is a narrow steep road. What happens if you meet another car?"

"One of the drivers has to back up until he reaches a spot where he can pull off the road and let the other fellow go by."

"That's some system. Suppose you get two drivers who won't back up?"

"Then they either sit there till one of them gives in, or they hit each other head on."

That was the last word either of them said until they came to the house. Owen brought the car to a stop, and a woman appeared, framed in the lighted front doorway. "Milton," she cried, "where have you been?"

"That's Mrs. Horowitz?"

Mr. Horowitz offered his hand. "Goodbye."

"But I'm not leaving yet," Owen answered, "I'd like to talk to your wife."

"Whatever you want to ask her, ask me, I'll tell you."

"I've already asked you," Owen replied softly, "and you said you didn't know." He was halfway across the grass before Mr. Horowitz was out of the car. "Good evening," Owen said, "I'm Owen Henderson, Mrs. Horowitz. If you wouldn't mind, I'd like to talk to you for a few minutes."

"Who are you?" Mrs. Horowitz peered out at him, inspecting him from head to toe. Her husband was at Owen's shoulder. "Riba," he barked, "go upstairs, I'll talk to him."

She paid no attention.

"I'm from the police. I'm the man who found your daughter."

She turned her head away from him. "Bernard! Bernard! Where are you?"

"Here I am," Bernard said from in back of her.

"Why do you hide like that?" she scolded. "Come with me, we have to talk to this man about Arlene."

"Riba!" Mr. Horowitz said, "I told you—"

"Come," she said, "we can talk in here." She led

130

Owen into the office, then turned around. "Not you, Milton," she said. "You had your chance with him, now it's my turn."

"If you think I'm going to let—"

"Milton," she said, her voice rising, "if you don't let me talk to him alone, I'll tell him things you don't even think I know, right in front of you. Now go, before I lose my temper. Don't worry. Bernard'll be here, he can report to you, won't you, Bernard?"

The boy's only response was a fierce scowl.

"All I wanted to ask," Owen began, just as embarrassed.

"Hush," Mrs. Horowitz commanded. "Wait. Not one word until he leaves." She waved her hands at her husband as though exorcising a ghost. "Out, out—" and pushed him toward the door and closed it after him. Then she opened it again quickly, screamed, "And don't try to listen at the keyhole, either," and slammed it shut.

"Now," she said courteously to Owen, "you were saying?"

"I wanted to check with you on whether or not Arlene had suffered from any kind of mental illness."

"Mental illness? What an idea! Certainly not."

Owen swallowed. "Thank you very much."

"Is that all?" She sounded disappointed. "Who told you she had, may I ask?"

"Mrs. Boardman said she'd been hospitalized—"

"Oh, *that*! She wasn't feeling so well once, you understand, but it was nothing, just a little upset. She got over it right away, in no time at all."

"Can you tell me her doctor's name, or the name of the hospital?"

She pondered. "Now, isn't that funny? I can't remember either one. Of course, I'm so confused right now it's a wonder I can even remember my own name."

"Bernard, do you—"

"No, no!" Mrs. Horowitz interceded promptly. "He wouldn't know. How would he know something like that, a boy his age?"

Bernard gazed at the floor, but said nothing.

"Yes," Owen finally echoed, "how?"

"Is that all?"

"Yes, I guess it is."

"Bernard, open the door for the policeman," Mrs. Horowitz ordered.

"Thank you, Bernard," Owen said, and went out into the hall, where Mr. Horowitz waited, leaning against the newel post, his face disastrous. When Mrs. Horowitz came out, Bernard lagging after her, he snapped at her, "Come upstairs, we have to pack up if we're going home first thing tomorrow morning."

"First thing? Why first thing?"

"Why should we stay longer? Are you enjoying it so much here we have to stay longer?" he shouted, trembling with fury. Miranda came into the hall.

"Please," she begged, "Couldn't you be quieter? They'll be able to hear everything you say down in the village."

"What about Arlene?" Mrs. Horowitz asked, her voice low and heavy with hate. "Have I come all this way, and I'm not to see my only daughter, my dead child?"

"What's the matter with you? I arranged to have the body sent home, it's already on the way."

"Sent home?"

"What do you want, to carry it back on the plane in your lap? Or in a suitcase?"

"Then why did I have to come here?"

"Because, you foolish woman, you wouldn't stay home like I told you to! Next time maybe you'll listen to me!" and he stamped up the narrow stairs to his bedroom.

Owen and Miranda had fled to the kitchen.

"Miranda," he whispered, "I owe you an apology."

"They are dreadful, aren't they?" she whispered back. He nodded agreement. "Owen, did you say anything about—you know?" He shook his head. "Whew! Thank you. That's very good of you. I don't think I could cope with any more scenes like that today."

Owen didn't want Miranda to think he'd done her a favor. "I was going to, but he made it impossible, there was no way I could get him to listen to me."

"I don't care why you didn't tell him, all I care about is that I won't have to discuss it with either of them right away."

"Were they this bad when you talked to them before?"

"I never met them till today. And Horace never saw them together, now that I think of it. First he only met the mother and Arlene. Then the father came here by himself in the spring to look at the camp. Horace volunteered to come to talk to him then because he said he was sure that Mr. Horowitz wouldn't be happy dealing with a woman."

"How did he know that?"

"I don't know. Probably something his cousin Clara told him. Anyway Horace did say he was difficult. Even so, I can assure you I would never have agreed to any special cabin's being built."

"I don't understand."

"The father said our practice cabins weren't good enough for his daughter, and if she was going to come here we'd have to let him make his own arrangements for her. And of course Horace gave in, and then conveniently forgot to tell me what was going on till it was too late to stop it. I should have known there was something the matter when he offered to pay so much extra."

"Extra what?"

"Extra tuition," she admitted. "He agreed to pay double if we'd come up a little early, and if we'd put up her New York teacher when he came here. And he paid it all in advance, too." She sighed. "Owen, I guess I'm being punished for greediness."

"Indeed?" Owen said softly. "Heartlessness might be more like it, Miranda."

"Heartless? For whom do you expect me to feel sorry? For them?"

"How about Arlene?"

"People must learn to face their problems, Owen, whatever they are, not run away from them. That girl chose to kill herself, nobody else had anything to do—I mean, she made that decision herself, and I can neither sympathize with it nor condone it."

"I see."

Horace came into the kitchen, and Owen said, "Oh, there you are. I've been wanting to see you all day."

"I've been right here, God knows." He put an empty glass into the sink and said wearily, "A little more of this, and I'm going on happy pills myself."

"I'd like to talk to you, Horace. Let's go outside." The two men walked out to Owen's car and leaned against the fender, surrounded by the soft resigned air with which the day announces that it's actually over, even though it isn't quite time for sunset yet.

"What can I do for you?"

"Did you know the Horowitzes before Arlene came here?"

"No. They're Chicago people."

"How did she hear about Roundmount?"

"My guess is they saw one of the ads, wrote for a brochure, and sent in a deposit. Mandy handles all that."

"You knew nothing about her before she came? You'd never seen her?"

"Oh, well, actually yes I did. I happened to be in Chicago and Mandy asked me to interview her and hear her play."

"Is that usual?"

"With people Mandy doesn't know, yes. She gets most of the people here through word of mouth, so there's usually some way to check up on them. Mandy doesn't like to take anybody who isn't serious. Especially instrumentalists. If they're not up to the level of the other students they don't have a good time."

"Anybody else in the family there when you talked to her?"

"Just the mother. She fed me a lot of nonsense about how big a genius her daughter was, which I didn't pay much attention to. Then I heard her play. I couldn't believe how good she was. You heard her, didn't you?"

"Yes. The other night. Fantastic technique."

"Especially for someone her age. She was a star, Owen. I could have made a fortune with her."

"Did you have any idea she was disturbed?"

"Well, of course, I've seen a few nuts in my time, most of them my clients. Very childish people, performers. They're all bananas, that's for openers. So she was strange, so what? So was her mother. It didn't bother me. Though I will say I had no idea she was crazy enough to kill herself."

"Miranda told you about the autopsy report?"

"Uh huh."

"I understand that you went to Benton's party?"

"Uh huh."

"You left about ten-thirty with Cathleen?"

"I walked her back to the dining hall. Mandy'd gone back earlier with that professor and his wife."

"I got a pretty full report about what happened at the party from the students. The only thing I want to know from you is, how did Benton act with Arlene?"

"Like he acts with every other woman. Including, I might add, my wife."

"Do you think he meant it seriously with Arlene?"

"Owen, if you're gradually getting around to asking me do I think he was the one who raped her, the answer is yes."

"Just like that—yes? Without qualifications?"

"Without any ifs, ands, or buts. Pin it on him, Owen, get him good, and put the sonofabitch away where he can't do any more harm. As far as I'm concerned, it'd be the best piece of work you could ever hope to do."

14

By the time Miranda was able to get the Horowitzes organized to go eat dinner, it was so late that almost everybody else was through. The students who were hanging around the outside of the lodge on the terrace and the steps, talking and laughing, all fell decorously silent as the five of them appeared, parting in front of them, Miranda thought, like the waves of the Red Sea. Inside they were also surrounded by respectful but distant regard, for Horace had passed the word around that the Horowitzes were too upset to want to meet anybody, and the faculty members who were still eating knew better than to come over to their table.

To Miranda's relief everybody behaved quite well. For one thing, Mrs. Horowitz's tranquilizers had finally caught up with her, and though she sat through the whole meal in an obvious stupor, barely able to eat, at least she kept quiet. Mr. Horowitz, understandably exhausted by what he'd been through that afternoon, was also subdued; and Bernard, of course, had nothing to say. Consequently there was little or no conversation until they'd reached coffee, when Mr. Horowitz, somewhat revived by the food, asked, "Say, where's that doctor you were talking about before, I'd like to see him."

"Doctor?" Miranda repeated, puzzled. "What doctor?"

"That psychiatrist from New York who was treating Arlene."

"I never said he was treating her," Miranda corrected him sharply. "He isn't here to treat anybody, he's studying painting."

"You implied that he was."

"I certainly did no such thing." Horace observed Mr. Horowitz purse his lips and blink, and guessed he was trying to assess Miranda's renewed confidence and firmness. Now that Mandy didn't have to worry any more about what Owen might tell them, she was obviously going to treat the Horowitzes like recalcitrant children, which was the way she usually managed difficult parents; and he wondered if Milton was going to let her get away with it.

"That reminds me," she went on smoothly, "before you leave we must settle a number of things."

"Such as?"

"What you want to do with Arlene's personal belongings? Her clothes, the piano, her music—and the horse."

"Horse?" Mrs. Horowitz rallied, though foggily. "What horse?"

"Arlene's horse. The one I bought her last spring when I came here to see about building that little house for her to practice in. You know, I told you."

"House? You mean, there's a house up here with a horse in it?"

"Riba, what's the matter with you?" He turned on his son. "How many of those things did you give her, for God's sake?"

"Two," Bernard answered sulkily. "That's what the

137

doctor said."

"Never mind, dear Mrs. Horowitz," Miranda said, and patted her hand. "We'll take care of it, don't worry."

"I hope so. What would I do with a horse in the house?"

"Will you have time to pack Arlene's things," Miranda asked, "or do you want me to take care of it for you? I'd be delighted to be of service."

"We can discuss that later," Mr. Horowitz said brusquely. "Before we do anything else, the first thing we'll have to settle is the tuition refund."

Chalk one up for old Milt, Horace thought.

"What time are we leaving tomorrow, Dad?" Bernard asked.

"I told the pilot to pick us up at the airport at ten-thirty. If that's all right with Mrs. Boardman."

"Perfectly. Breakfast is at eight-thirty, which'll give us plenty of time to get there." She looked around the table. "If we're through, why don't we—"

On their way out, Bernard walked so slowly that the other four left the dining room ahead of him. He stopped in front of one of the student paintings which were being exhibited on the dining room walls, and studied it, his hands in his pockets, his shoulders hunched, his round head, with its already thinning black hair, cocked to one side. Dave Haller was sitting nearby over a final cup of coffee, and he smiled at Bernard's inspection. "Do you like it?" he asked.

Bernard answered him very seriously. "No, not at all."

"Why not?"

"It's not a good painting."

"Why not?"

"It's derivative, and I don't think the person who painted it understands fully what the man he copied

138

from wanted to do."

"And you do?"

"I didn't say that. Why bring me into it or what I understand? All I said was I don't think that this particular artist understands the principles behind abstract expressionism, and so it's a bad painting."

"Never mind this particular artist," Dave said, and shoved a chair toward him with his foot. 'Sit down and tell me what you think the principles of abstract expressionism are."

Bernard shook his head. "I can't. I have to stay with my mother and father."

"You're Arlene's brother, then?"

"Yes."

"My name's Haller, I teach art here. Everybody— we're all very sorry about what happened."

"Thank you." Horace appeared in the doorway and beckoned. "Bernard," he called, "your mother—"

"I'm coming." He looked at Dave. "Can I depend on you? Will you do me a favor?"

"I don't know," Dave answered. "What is it?"

Bernard took a folded paper out of his jacket pocket and thrust it into Dave's hand. "Give this to that big policeman who was here today, the one who said he found my sister. It's very important. Will you?"

"Yes," Dave said. "That I can promise you I'll do."

"And you won't give it to anybody else?"

"No, only to him."

"Thanks." He hurried across to the door, and out. Dave unfolded the paper and looked at it. Written on it, in a minute but thoroughly legible hand was: Dr. Harold Sherman, Hill Center for Psychotherapy, Chicago. Escaped 11/21, recaptured 3/16. Released 6/18.

15

Dear Mr. Henderson:

I am replying to your letter of June 20th with regard to the death of Arlene Horowitz. Thank you for letting me hear about this, and for being so frank with me about the details.

In view of the distressing circumstances surrounding her suicide, I feel justified in complying with your request, and will at once forward to Dr. Agnew a transcript of her case record. As for your question about its inevitability, I cannot in all good conscience answer it either yes or no. First of all, because placing ultimate blame is not my province. I only deal with and try to patch up the end results of years of small separate personal misfortunes, each of which contributes its quota to a particular situation, and each of which must be evaluated accordingly. And in the second place, even if I wanted to, I couldn't, because I simply have no way to tell.

Yours truly,
Harold Sherman, M.D.

HS:jlm
cc: Dr. Ezra Agnew

Dear Ezra,

It's good to be in touch with you again after all the years that have passed since we were residents together—more years than I care to count or you either, probably. I've heard about you now and then through the grapevine, though, and I'm sorry to have had those rumors about your divorce confirmed. Better luck next time.

I'm sending you a complete transcript of the Horowitz records. Please return it when you've finished using it. Naturally it will have to be up to you how much of it to show to Mr. Henderson, since you're the only one who's familiar with the situation there and with his particular qualifications for understanding its contents.

Arlene wasn't my patient for very long, as you will see, but during the short time she was under treatment here she made extremely rapid strides toward recovery. Although I am well aware that one can never tell about schizophrenics, I must confess I made the mistake of allowing myself to feel optimistic about her case. Perhaps I was kidding myself about being able to save her, and merely indulging my own fantasies of omnipotence, but after all, considering it took those parents of hers eighteen years to drive her to an open break, I think it's fair to say that she possessed truly remarkable stamina and had exhibited an almost heroic degree of resistance in the past. That was one of the reasons why I thought she might be able to show permanent improvement in the future. No other patient I've ever had wanted so much to get well, or was as determined to do it, and I think that if she'd been given adequate shelter and support away from her family for the next couple of years, she might very well have pulled herself out of it almost entirely. It's pretty obvious now that without help she was doomed.

Ezra, there simply wasn't anything else I could do. Believe me, I tried as hard as I could to keep her here, but her family—mostly her father, although he had considerable covert support from the mother, who kept saying she wanted to help, but who actually managed very efficiently to sabotage almost all of Arlene's struggles to help herself—insisted on taking her home in spite of all my best efforts to persuade them otherwise. I've faced similar situations before, as I'm sure you have, too, and we'll undoubtedly both have to face them again, but just between us, losing this one was tough on me. Her suicide is a tragedy for many, many reasons. For one thing, there aren't too many people around with her kind of talent, and in my judgment the world has been deprived of somebody who had the potential to become a tremendously creative individual.

As ever,
Hal

Encl.

CASE RECORD

Horowitz, Arlene

Admission and Initial Interview:

The patient, a well-nourished white female, aged 18, was admitted to the hospital on November 21 at 4:15 p.m. She was accompanied by her mother, brother , and the referring family physician, Dr. Arthur Steiner of Chicago.

The patient was in a highly emotional state, crying, disoriented, incoherent, and disheveled and dirty. When taken to her room, she immediately stripped the bed, threw the sheets and blankets in a heap on the floor, and crouched in the corner of the room furthest from the door. She was otherwise not violent, however, and submitted passively, though tearfully, to the attempts of the doctor and nurse to make her comfortable. A sedative was administered, and the patient almost immediately fell asleep.

The mother, who was also very excited and tearful, stated that the patient had refused to leave her bedroom for the last three days except to go to the bathroom. The patient also had refused to speak to anyone who came into the room during that time, although she carried on long, animated, and loud conversations with hallucinated companions that frequently degenerated into screaming arguments. During her monologues the patient often claimed that designs made up of musical notes were being pasted on the bedroom walls. She became especially distraught whenever she saw them there, and would climb on the bed and try to scrub them away with her hands, invariably beginning to cry and lament when she couldn't get them off.

Sometime during these three days the patient's hair, which is very long and unkempt, was dyed bright green. The mother stated that she didn't know how or when this had been done, but thought maybe the patient might have used ink to do it with since she had found two empty bottles that had once held green ink on the floor under the patient's bed.

During the last three days the patient has also refused to eat anything. She fought vigorously all efforts made by her mother to force-feed her, and when her mother did succeed once in making her swallow some soup, the patient promptly vomited. The mother states that this refusal to eat was the main reason why she called the doctor. "I knew there must be something really wrong with her," she said. "My Arlene was never a picky eater."

The referring physician confirmed most of the mother's statements about this three-day acute episode. He was called in yesterday afternoon (November 20th), and spent many hours trying to persuade the mother to commit the patient. Before he could get her to agree to do it, he said, he had to threaten to call in the police and have her (the mother) arrested for abusing her child. The mother finally gave in under this pressure, but the physician said he was sure that if the father hadn't been away, there would have been no chance at all of ever getting the patient out of the house. He reported that once he had explained to the patient where he wanted to take her, she dressed and left her room and the house with little or no protest.

The patient is described by the physician, who has known her since her infancy, as an extraordinarily intelligent and talented girl around whom the family life has always revolved. The patient's life, in turn, has been spent almost entirely in developing her musical gift, which is considerable. According to Dr. Steiner, she has never been allowed to have any friends her own age, but has spent most of her time with her mother, either playing the piano, or studying music. She has been educated privately by tutors and by her mother, and has never attended public school.

Dr. Steiner said that in his opinion the patient has been "acting crazy" for some time, and reported that she had disappeared for two or three days at a time on at least four occasions that he knew of during the previous eighteen months. He knew about these fugues because her mother brought the patient in to see him for a physical check-up after each one, and he felt that the patient had been noticeably more disturbed each time he'd seen her. He was unable to obtain any further history because the mother invariably insisted on accompanying her daughter into the examining room, and immediately interrupted any and all attempts to discuss the patient's problems. The physician stated that try as he might, he was unable to prevent this surveillance, because the mother was so completely determined. The mother confirmed the occurrence of the fugues, but only reluctantly, stating that she felt they were "nothing to worry about, so why talk about them?"

The patient's father, a wealthy manufacturer of textile machinery, is reported as having left last week on an extended business trip through Europe and the Orient, and is not expected home for at least three months. The patient's only sibling, a boy two and a half years younger than she, was present at the initial interview, but it was impossible to get a statement from him because the mother answered any questions that he was asked before he had a chance to reply. On the way out, however, the brother did manage to whisper to the admitting physician that his sister was very unhappy, and he hoped there was something the hospital would be able to do to help her.

Tentative Diagnosis: Schizophrenia

Ezra thumbed past the sheaf of closely-typed staff reports, the results of the medical and clinical tests, and the memos of staff conferences, until he came to Hal's notes on his analytic sessions with Arlene. He skimmed through these, concentrating mostly on the weekly summary sheets; he paid particular attention to the final session, dated March 16th.

The patient was seen an hour earlier than usual today so that she could be ready to leave with her family when they called for her. She was depressed and sad. She didn't want to go with them, because she knew she'd get well faster if she stayed in the hospital, but she said she knew she had no alternative. She asked again if it would be possible for her to write now and then to tell me what was happening to her. When I assured her that I would always be pleased to hear from her, and that I would certainly continue to take an interest in her progress, she cheered up a little, although she was still far from delighted at the idea of leaving. What she dreaded most, she said, was the prospect of being unable to withstand her parents' hostility, both her father's direct and obviously aggressive bossing and her mother's more subtle, but just as destructive, competitive manipulation. "I don't want to be shoved around any more, but I'm not sure I'm strong enough yet to fight back without help." I reminded her that now at least she had some insight into the reasons for her father's hostility toward her, and she agreed. Even so, she remarked, that didn't make him any pleasanter, or any easier for her to handle. The patient left the hospital at 10:15 without exhibiting undue excitement or anxiety. The family physician will continue medication and follow up, and report any significant development.

Prognosis: Without enough insight yet to understand the reasons underlying her own ambivalence, the patient will undoubtedly continue to feel extremely threatened by any action that at all resembles or that can be construed by her as resembling her father's basically incestuous aggression. In the absence of any shield against this kind of pressure, the prognosis can only be doubtful or negative. The best that can be hoped for is that the patient will stabilize at her present very precarious level of functioning, which she maintains, even with constant therapeutic reassurance and support, only at the expense of considerable psychic energy.

Frowning, Ezra turned this last sheet of paper over to put it on the top of the pile of the others that he'd read through. He noticed a few lines scribbled on the back of it in pencil, and picked it up again.

3/21: Tel. conv. with Dr. Steiner re poss. of getting Mr. H. to send A.H. away for summer, either to school or music camp. He agreed to broach subject with family.

4/1: Tel. conv. with Dr. Steiner: he reports Hs. receptive to music camp idea for A, because she refuses to practice as much as she should at home.

4/16: Tel. conv. with Dr. S. A.H. to be sent to camp in Conn. in return for promise to study hard and prepare for N.Y. debut in fall. Not much, but better than nothing.

Why, that poor bastard, Ezra thought pityingly. No wonder he had to make such a pitch to me about doing his best. And no wonder he had to hedge on Owen's question. He's partly responsible for her being here in the first place.

16

Arlene's belongings vanished from her room in the dorm almost before the Horowitzes had left the campus. That same day, too, the school, with relief, lurched back into its regular routine, and the gossip began to die down as the students once more got involved in their own concerns. But when the appearance of the revised schedules for the Sunday concerts on all the bulletin boards caused talk, particularly among the musicians who had been chosen to replace Arlene on the programs, Miranda reluctantly decided it would be better to wait a while before she packed and shipped the things in Arlene's cabin. Selling the horse had been taken care of by Mr. Horowitz personally; he'd made her stop at the stable on their way to the airport so he'd be sure, by doing the bargaining himself, to get a price he considered satisfactory. She picked a gray and rainy day to finally start on the job, and right after breakfast slipped out the back door and through the garden into the field.

Head bent, shoulders hunched against the light but persistent downpour, she tramped up the hill. The grass on either side of the path was almost knee high and would be ready to be hayed in a couple of days. The hem of her yellow oilskin slicker brushed against the pale blue-green seed tips of the stalks, knocking off drops of clear chilly water, a few of which trickled down her bare legs into her boots. As she had hoped, nobody else was out. There was very little stirring altogether. She saw a single red-winged blackbird swaying on the thin stem of a bush, his fluffed-out wet plumage looking frayed and tacky; one small brown rabbit, who dodged ahead of her up the path, then disappeared into the landscape. Both of them looked as sodden and depressed as she was beginning to feel, squelching along through the wet.

She regarded the cabin, when she came in view of it, with resentment and disfavor. She'd never liked it. Mr. Horowitz's taste was too rich for her blood, too pretentious by far for the standard of sturdy, uncomfortable, plain make-do which, in her mind, was one of the important philosophical contributions Roundmount had to offer to its students, many of whom had not had the good fortune to be born in New England. She stopped under a pine tree to look at it, and the idea came to her that perhaps it might be worthwhile to build on a small kitchen so that they could rent the place out for the summer; she'd have to talk to the contractor about it. No point in letting a perfectly good building go to waste. Or maybe they could leave it the way it was and use it to sleep important visitors, as a kind of guest cabin. While she was debating these choices in her mind, the wind shifted into her face, and she became aware that somebody was playing the piano in the cabin. Frowning, she hurried forward, her boots slipping and squeaking against the wet ground. The closer she got to the house and the more clearly the music came to her ears, the more convinced she was that it was Arlene who was playing. And not merely playing, either, but practicing; for, apparently displeased with the way one particular phrase sounded, she stopped and went over it a number of times, first more slowly, then gradually faster and faster until it was up to tempo, before she went on. Continually repeating to herself that she was being ridiculous, that it *couldn't* be Arlene, but knowing all the same that it was, that there *was* no other pianist at the camp who was remotely capable of playing

149

so well, Miranda reached the cabin practically at a run. Panting, she flung open the door, and with the same motion reached around inside and switched on the light. The slim figure sitting on the piano bench turned around to face her, gazing toward her with unseeing eyes.

"*Martin*!"

"Hi, Mandy." He blinked at her, scowling in the light.

"What do you think you're doing? Who told you you could—"

"I'm not hurting anything," he said sullenly. "I've been listening to Arlene play, that's all."

"Turn that thing *off*!" Miranda leaned against the door jamb and pulled off her boots, then stepped inside in her bare feet. With very bad grace Martin went over and shut off the tape. She took off her slicker and kerchief, shook most of the water off the coat outside, then brought her things in and hung them on a hook behind the door. Drops of rain ran down the coat and fell onto the quarry tile floor, making a little round puddle.

"It's freezing in here," she said, her voice a little less hostile. "Let's have a fire." She padded across the floor, knelt in front of the fireplace, and deftly built and lit one, using wood and kindling from the wicker woodbasket. "What're you doing out on a day like this, anyway?" she asked over her shoulder.

"I couldn't stay home, it was too gloomy, so I came down here." He paced back and forth behind her without offering to help.

She turned and glanced up at him, and asked, suddenly concerned, "Martin, do you feel all right? What's the matter with you, you look—haven't you been sleeping, or what? You look absolutely exhausted."

"I'm all right."

"Are you sure?" She stood up and came over to put her hand on his forehead. "You look as if you might be feverish." He jerked his head away from her touch.

"I'm all right, I tell you," he replied irritably, and ran his hand over the stubble on his chin. "What're *you* doing out on a day like this? Why're *you* here?"

"You sound as if you think I had no right to come," she said, annoyed. Martin ignored the challenge and merely stared at her. "I'm supposed to pack Arlene's things," she finally explained, "and have them shipped back to her family."

"What're her folks like?"

"Unbelievable, simply unbelievable." Miranda looked around the room. She was blessed with an inordinate ability to concentrate, and the mere act of focusing her attention on the job she'd come to do meant that she immediately grew much less conscious of Martin. He'd finally stopped prowling and was slumped in one of the armchairs, his legs straight out in front of him resting on his heels, his chin on his chest, his hands in his pockets.

"How are they unbelievable?"

"Unbelievably awful, that's how." Miranda decided she'd begin with the music, since that was the easiest. She sat down crosslegged on the floor next to the piano, and began to collect and pile the books and single pieces of music into neat stacks.

"What makes them so awful?"

"Ohh—" she answered, impatient with his interruptions, "they are. Her father's a monster and a bully, and the old lady's as nutty as her daughter, if not nuttier."

"Arlene was not nutty." The intensity underlying his denial penetrated even Miranda's withdrawal, and she looked up. "Martin," she asked, "are you *sure* you feel all right?"

151

"Why can't you leave me alone? I'm perfectly fine, I told you." Rebuffed, she went back to stacking.

"How's your work going?" she asked.

"It's not," he informed her. He got up and paced a little more. "I'm going to hear the rest of this tape," he announced belligerently, and turned the recorder on again. The middle section of the Chopin *Bacarolle* filled the room.

"Not so loud," Miranda directed. He turned the volume down a little, and went back to the armchair to listen with half-closed eyes. Miranda couldn't help herself. She was compelled to stop what she was doing. "God, she was good," she murmured when the piece was over.

"What happened to her, Miranda?" Martin asked, just as softly, "What made her kill herself?"

"How should I know?" Miranda replied, immediately wary. "I'm no psychiatrist."

For a few seconds the only sounds in the room were the soft slap of the music being piled one piece on top of another, and the hiss of the tape feeding through the blocks. Then all at once Arlene was speaking. As Miranda and Martin stared at one another, her light clear voice said, "Dear Doctor Hal, this is Arlene Horowitz. How are you? I've wanted to write you a long time ago but there really hasn't been anything important to tell you, I guess, so I haven't bothered you. I'm spending the summer at Roundmount, it's a music and art camp in the Berkshires. Dr. Steiner was the one who suggested I ought to go away someplace for the summer, and Clara, Daddy's secretary, knew about this camp, so Mommy and Daddy decided it was okay for me to spend the summer here. I was kind of surprised how little fuss they made about it, though that's not really fair, I suppose, sometimes they do let me do what I want. Anyway, here I am, and I'm going to send you

152

this tape instead of a letter, all right? Daddy bought me this machine so I could listen to myself play, and I thought as long as it's here, I can use it to talk to you besides. He'd be furious if he knew I was using it for this instead of practicing, wouldn't he? But it's so much easier to talk like this than to write, almost as though it's a regular session like I used to have with you in the hospital. I never seem to be able to say everything I mean when I write, can you? But now I can tell you about Roundmount, and what's been happening to me since I got here a few weeks ago. I've been practicing like a good little girl [she gave the soft giggle Martin remembered so clearly]. I've got my own piano up here for the summer, and that makes it a lot easier for me, because it's something I'm used to. I played some Chopin for you on the first part of this tape, and I think I've improved a lot recently, don't you?"

The tape ran silent for almost half a minute, and Miranda sighed and relaxed, only to stiffen again as Arlene came back on.

"Doctor Hal," [her voice trembled as though she had trouble controlling her breath, and the words hurried along] "there's somebody up here—a man—I don't know if I can describe him the right way so I can—I don't know if I can tell you exactly what he's like or why he's so important all of a sudden, when I've only seen him two or three times. He teaches writing here, and he's—Doctor Hal, I think what it is, he's kind of like my father. Only he's not so old, of course, and he's got a beard, and he's terribly handsome and attractive. I think he likes me. The other night we ate dinner at Miranda's—she's the one who runs the school—together, and after dinner, he came after me when I left the dining room—"

Miranda pivoted on her hip and stretched toward the machine to turn it off. Before her hand could touch the

153

switch, Martin had flung himself out of his chair and was crouching over her with such fury on his face that her hand dropped and she shrank away from him. "Leave her alone!" he commanded hoarsely. "Let her say what she wants to!"

"Martin—?" Miranda whispered. "What—?"

"—and then, after I got away, he walked out of the house and slammed the door, just like Daddy does. You know, the way you made me see that every time I don't do what he wants, he shows his disapproval by refusing to love me? The thing is, I felt just the same way when I heard Roger—his name's Roger—walk out then. Doctor Hal, I want him to like me, and yet I'm afraid of him, too. What do you think? Should I pay a lot of attention to him and let him know I like him? Or should I try to make believe he's not around? Or should I make him leave me alone? I don't know what to do. I want to do all three of those things, really. I felt so funny when he put his hand on my arm, just as if I didn't have any will of my own, and I got all quivery inside—and yet, I didn't like it at the same time. I know you said you'd never tell me what to do, but please, couldn't you at least write me what you think, or send me a message on tape like this? It would probably help." She gave a ragged sigh, and her voice became firmer.

"As far as the rest of the people up here are concerned, they're all right but I don't care much one way or the other about them. There's a man named Martin, from New York, who's got a summer house here, a cabin in the woods. He acts awful scared, but he's okay. There's Cathleen, who used to be an opera singer. She looks like the witch from Snow White, and she keeps raving about the beauty of vocal theater. Boring. There's a real doctor named Ezra something, and Janice, who's divorced, and who's a friend of Roger's I think. And Horace and Miranda. They're married. Miranda runs

154

this place, and she's awful bossy.

"Nobody here knows anything about music at all, but maybe when the rest of the people come up next week there'll be somebody I can talk to. I hope so.

"The main thing I'm worried about though is Roger, and that's mostly why I'm sending you this. Doctor Hal, actually he's not very nice, and I don't like him, so why can he make me feel so funny, why do I keep looking for him all day long and think about him so much almost all the time? I want to run away from him and not have anything to do with him. I feel like I ought to, somehow. Yet, for some reason, I don't know why—I don't think I can."

The voice stopped and the tape came to an end. Martin got up and walked across the room, and stood with his back to Miranda, looking into the fireplace. Miranda reached over and turned off the machine. Still sitting on the floor, she said, "I don't understand what's come over you."

"Well, it bothers me!" He hit the paneling over the fireplace with his fist.

"There's no need to shout like that, I can hear you perfectly well, I'm right here in the room." She came over to stand next to him. "What bothers you?"

"The fact that it doesn't bother you!" he said, almost weeping. "That nobody cares, not even you. That nobody will do anything."

"I don't know what you're talking about."

"About what we just heard on that tape. Roger. He killed her. You know it as well as me. Why are you letting him get away with it? Why don't you do something, why doesn't Owen do something? It's not fair!"

Miranda walked to an armchair, sat down, and lit a cigarette. She tucked her legs up on the seat sideways, sliding her bare feet under her skirt, and massaged her cold toes through the fabric. That damn kid, she thought, she's caused me nothing but trouble, first with Owen, then with Roger, and now this. Aloud, her voice deliberate and reasonable, she said, "Aren't you jumping to conclusions?"

"Am I?" He swung around. "I don't think so."

"I do. I don't know where you get the idea that Roger had anything to do with her death. There isn't anything on that tape to say he was the reason she killed herself."

"Are you trying to tell me that nothing happened between them, that he didn't rape her?"

She puffed on her cigarette and looked him in the eye. "Not as far as I know, he didn't."

"Don't lie to me, Mandy!"

"I'm not lying. Have I ever lied to you?" He didn't answer, and she pursued her advantage. "You know I haven't, you know I hate liars. And something else I hate is an unjust accusation, and that's what you're making against Roger." She held up her hand. "Don't interrupt me till I'm through," she ordered. "I'll admit I knew when they first met that—well, that Roger liked her, let's put it that way. But when I explained to him that it would not be wise for him to get involved, he stopped. Now I know Roger enjoys having girls make a fuss over him, but he's not—most of the time, there's nothing to it. And what you don't know is that after Arlene—after her tragic—well, anyway, I asked him pointblank if he—he'd made love to her, and he said no he hadn't, and I believe him. So I don't quite see what you expect me to do. Am I supposed to fire a man and ruin his teaching career simply because a crazy, spoiled kid who had a crush on him drowned herself? It wasn't his fault, it's not as if he'd done anything to—"

"He did, he did!"

Miranda crushed out her butt and stood up. "Martin, if you think you know something about this, I suggest you tell Owen. Right away."

"Mandy, he—"

"No," she said, moving toward the door, picking up her boots and slipping her feet into them. "Don't tell me. Because as far as I'm concerned, it's a waste of time to discuss this any further." And with that she gathered up her slicker and was gone.

He ran to the door and flung it open. Miranda was moving away down the hill, huddling herself into her coat. "Mandy, come back!" he yelled. Unheeding, she disappeared into the trees at the edge of the field. He stared after her, leaning out of the open doorway until his head and shoulders were wet. Finally he retreated into the cabin, closed and locked the door after himself, and switched off the lights. Shivering under his cold wet shirt, muttering incoherently about betrayal, he crossed to the recorder, crouched over it, rewound the tape, and pushed the Play button. The tape started its smooth forward glide. He sat down on the hearth, crossed his arms on his knees, and rested his head on them, waiting, his eyes shut, for Arlene to play for him once again the first sensuously langorous statement of the theme of the *Bacarolle*.

About three o'clock that same day, Ezra went over to the potting shed to talk to Janice. She looked up from her work and smiled a welcome at him. The mist had collected in his uncovered hair, and in the light his head sparkled as though it were outlined in tiny crystal beads.

"Hi. All you need's a trident and a conch," she said, "and you could pass for Neptune risen from the sea."

"I believe Neptune sometimes has horns, too," he replied. He looked startled, then laughed. "Well, well. I thought I'd gotten over my wife's infidelity, but I see I haven't."

"Oh honestly, Ezra," Janice said, instantly cross.

157

"Don't you ever stop practicing?"

"Not on me, how can I? What's the good of spending all that time and trouble developing a third ear if I keep it deaf to what I say myself?"

"I thought public self-analysis went out with the salon."

"Okay, okay. Next time I won't say anything out loud, I promise."

"The thing is—"

"You think I analyze you all the time, too, like that—is that what's bothering you?" She nodded. "To some extent I do, I can't help it anymore than you can help viewing a person's bone structure as though it were sculpture or looking at me half-drowned and seeing Neptune, which is both an artistic and a literary image. But I try very hard to keep my conclusions unconscious, if that's any consolation. Anyway, this session of salon analysis—" they both grinned "—isn't why I came over. I spoke to Owen this morning. He's having some people in to play chamber music tonight and he invited us to come and listen. I took the liberty of accepting for both of us."

"Wonderful. I'd love to go."

"He's coming to pick Maura up about seven-thirty—she's playing—and he'll take us down with—"

The door opened and Miranda came in. She greeted them, but barely, went over to the counter, and started to rummage through the drawers where the modeling tools were kept.

"What're you looking for?" Janice asked. "Maybe have it over here."

"One of my boning knives."

"One of your what?"

"My boning knives," she repeated impatiently. "One of them's gone from the rack in the kitchen where belongs. I thought maybe somebody might've brought

158

out here.'' She banged the drawer shut. ''Maybe it's in the art shed.''

''Why would you look for it there?''

''I don't know, mostly because I've looked everyplace else, I guess.'' She walked around the shed. ''Maybe when Horace—'' Her eye lit on three clay pots set out on the counter. ''Whose pots are these?''

''Hannah's. She threw them yesterday.''

''But they're wet.''

''She came back a little while ago and dipped them in underglaze.''

''Stupid! She got them too wet. This big one's collapsed.''

Janice went over and looked. ''That's too bad. It's a nice pot. Or was.''

''I think I can still save it.'' Miranda reached under the sink and picked up a batt from the top of the pile.

''Save it? It's not your pot! Let her make her own mistakes.''

''Mind your own business.'' Miranda put the batt back and took a deep breath. ''Oh, dear, I am sorry, Janice. I'm so jumpy and irritable today. It must be this rotten weather that's making me so depressed. You're right of course. Please forgive me.''

''Of course. We all feel depressed, I think. Ever since—''

''Ever since,'' Ezra finished the sentence for her, ''Arlene died.''

17

Owen's mother welcomed them graciously. She was a short, plump woman, with clear hazel eyes and fair skin, like her son's; she must have been quite a handsome woman, Janice thought, when she was younger and her hair, now gray, had been dark. She and Maura greeted one another with much affection and a flurry of "My dear, how well you look," and "I'm so glad to see you again, how have you been?" While they were exchanging compliments, Owen said, "We're playing in here," and led Janice and Ezra into a high-ceilinged Victorian double parlor, a fifty-foot expanse of parquet flooring, oriental rugs, and off-white walls, entirely open except for four graceful fluted columns supporting an ornately carved foot-deep molding that delineated the space into two rooms. A piano and the inevitable metal music stands and folding chairs were grouped at the far end of the second room, and a number of comfortable chairs had been arranged for an audience in the first room.

Owen introduced them to the people who were already there: Frank Burch and his wife Gloria, their daughter Eleanor, and a young man, Gerald Evans, who was rather obviously attached to Eleanor. Then Emily Henderson, still talking, came in with Maura. Maura knew everybody except the Evans boy, and a conversation began which dealt mostly with people who had been at Roundmount during previous summers, and who hadn't come back. Janice and Ezra, completely excluded by this gossip, drew a little closer together, and were rescued by Owen, who took them into the second parlor, where he made them drinks and chatted with them about the house, until the doorbell rang and he excused himself to answer it.

Sipping their drinks, Ezra and Janice looked around. Both parlors boasted shallow squared-off bays with cushioned seats under long narrow windows. Curious to see the grounds, the two of them skirted the piano and a cello lying on the floor on its side, and went over to look outside.

The Hendersons' yard ran into the neighboring property without a break—neither hedge nor fence—so that in front of them stretched about three acres of uneven, hilly lawn, dotted with flowering shrubs and trees, and a number of small, well-tended flower plots. To their right, a continuous stone wall separated both lawns from the street; in several places the wall curved in around the row of huge elms that lined the road. Janice looked to the left, toward the back of the house, where a great maple shaded a small screened-in back porch. Beneath the tree, croquet wickets had been laid out on a flat piece of rather sparse grass. Beyond that was the garage, against whose pale brick wall some pear trees had been espaliered. The narrow pointed leaves on the obedient branches turned and twisted in the breeze, the raindrops winking in the light. What a setting for a piece of sculpture, she thought, and sighed without realizing it. Ezra touched her arm. "Let's go into the other room," he said. "We have to be introduced again."

Four of the five people who had come into the parlor were carrying instrument cases: one cello, one violin, a viola, and an oblong box too big for an oboe, Janice thought, probably a clarinet. The cellist was a white-haired, stooped, gentle-looking man, with a Viennese accent, Hans Ullman; his wife, Gerta, was the violist. The clarinetist was a handsome stocky blonde boy, Noel Janowitz; he and Maura started to exchange amiably teasing insults the minute they saw one another. The violinist was Madge Pallis, a skinny middle-aged woman whose straight bobbed black hair, bangs, dress, and manner were all right out of the twenties. The fifth person, the non-musician, was an Indian. Janice was so enchanted by the magnificent composition in black and white he presented: dark jacket, white shirt, golden-dark skin, white teeth and eyeballs, all set off against the white walls, that she wasn't concentrating when Owen introduced them, and never did learn his name.

As soon as the social amenities of introductions and drinks had been met, Mrs. Henderson said, "Well—shall we?" The seven musicians filed into the second parlor to unpack and tune their instruments, and the audience settled into its chairs. Mrs. Henderson, it appeared, played the piano, and to Janice's surprise, Owen played the cello. They looked through the music together, trying to decide what to play. "Why don't we begin with a string trio?" Madge asked.

"We have two celli—we could play the Schubert C Major Quintet," Gerta suggested.

"Oh, but let's not *start* with that, Schatzi," her husband said, and Owen smiled. "No," he agreed, "let's not."

"How about the Brahms Clarinet Quintet?" Maura asked. "That is, if Noel's up to it."

"I certainly am, if you are," Noel answered at once.

"Oh, well, *I* only have to play second violin, and that's no problem."

"Tell you what," Madge offered, "if we're going to do it, you can play first, Maura."

"Oh, no," Maura replied, laughing. "Thanks a lot."

Eventually they decided to warm up with a couple of Haydn quartets; Hans and Noel and Mrs. Henderson came and sat down, and the four instrumentalists who were to play got out their music, arranged themselves, raised their bows, looked at Madge, who bent her body forward to give them the downbeat, and the evening began.

It was not a demanding quartet. Besides, the clarity and the elegance of the classical idiom were so familiar to her that the music was immediately available on its own terms, and so Janice had nothing to do but enjoy it. At the beginning she listened without any thought but

162

pleasure; then her eye was taken by the patterns that the tips of the waving bows made in the lights, and the shadows they cast on the polished floor, and for a while she watched that. In the adagio, when the individual instruments could be easily distinguished, and the melodic path each took was fairly obvious, she closed her eyes and traced the rise and fall of the lines in her mind— light for the violins against dark, and dark for the viola and cello against light—until the skeins got so tangled she couldn't follow them anymore, and she relapsed into pure pleasure again. During the last movement she allowed herself to watch Owen. He sat on the edge of his chair, his big body straight, his head bent, his lower lip caught between his teeth, his face absorbed and intent; his legs, sprawled out on either side of the cello, were so long that his knees practically touched the floor, and his feet, supported on the tips of his shoes, reached past the back legs of the chair. Her fantasies about him were interrupted by the imperious drive of the finale, and she shared in Haydn's joy at the way the musical problem he'd set himself was being so neatly resolved.

As soon as the musicians were through, they looked at one another and smiled, pleased with Haydn, gratified with themselves and the sounds they'd made working together. Barely hearing or acknowledging the applause, they at once began to criticize their performance. Gerta commented on a way that the interpretation of the finale could be varied, and Madge said, "All right, let's play it over and see how it sounds." They replayed the last pages—whatever differences there were between the two performances escaped Janice—and then discussed which was preferable. Owen and Hans exchanged seats. It was decided that Mrs. Henderson should have a chance to warm up, and a Beethoven trio was substituted for the second quartet; so Maura sat out too. After the trio it was Noel's turn.

He noodled for a few minutes while the rest of them stretched and walked around, Owen returned to play the cello, and Mrs. Henderson sat out. Maura's half-hearted protests were overruled, and she was persuaded to play first for the Brahms, so she and Madge switched places. Noel fingered rapidly over a portion of his solo, and complained, "No matter how I try, I can never count this out right the first time."

"Are we ready?" Maura looked around.

"How fast are we going to take this?" Owen asked.

"You know me, I'm always in favor of slow tempi," Maura replied. "It's up to Noel, anyway."

"How about this?" Noel played a few measures, and everybody nodded. "Okay then, here we go." He took a deep breath and started the free-flowing rhapsodic introduction to the Brahms Clarinet Quintet.

Because it was less familiar to her, this music required attention, and Janice listened hard all the way through. Its cloudy wavering lushness was peremptory enough to have defeated all but the most determined efforts to ignore it, and when the quintet was over, it was not only the musicians who were glad to get up and stretch and walk around to relax. Partly in reaction to Brahms' long-sustained tensions, everybody began to talk at once, mainly about music and musicians. In the course of conversation Janice discovered that the Ullmans were both professional musicians, that Noel was a graduate student in physics, and that Madge was a writer. The Indian remained a mystery because he was involved in a quiet exchange with Eleanor and Gerald on the other side of the room. She and Madge fell into a conversation about people they both knew in publishing. Janice had had so many similar discussions so often that she was too bored by it to give Madge her full attention, and with half an ear eavesdropped on what the others were saying:

"I went to that farewell concert he gave last season at Carnegie Hall, and the next day after I saw the reviews I called him up, poor old man, and he said to me, 'It's funny, Hans, I'm right back where I started,' and I asked him what did he mean, and he said, 'Well, when I began playing in public I was only nine, you know, and everybody used to say then, "Doesn't he play very well for his age?" and now, fifty-eight years later, they're saying the same thing all over again'."

"I think he's with the Peace Corps now, training kids to go build roads or something. He couldn't get a leave of absence, so he simply—"

"—they went on a two-piano tour together, and got married while they were in Boston, kind of a keyboard romance."

"I haven't seen her since the Book Awards luncheon, where she was dressed in some kind of orange *thing*, my dear, you honestly couldn't call it anything else—"

"I bought it in, of all places, Syracuse. A dealer up there'd got hold of it from an estate, and a friend of mine happened to have his own instrument in the shop being repaired, and he tried it and called me, and I flew up there and bought it. It's such a beautiful instrument. Just look at that purfling, have you ever seen anything so lovely? There's supposed to be a brother violin someplace in New York, but so far I haven't—"

All this hubbub came to a stop coincidentally, except one conversation. In the lull, everybody was able to hear Hans Ullman say to Maura, "By the way, Gelman told me you have a remarkably gifted pianist at Roundmount this summer, a girl—what's her name, Schatzi?" he asked his wife, who supplied it without hestitation. "Oh, yes, that's it, Arlene Horowitz. Will she be playing on Sunday, do you know? Gelman was so enthusiastic I'm looking forward to hearing her."

"*Oh*!" Maura's embarrassment was so obvious and

so painful that Janice and Ezra and Owen, with one impulse, said together, "I'm afraid—But she's—Haven't you—" and then, of course, everybody did stare. Owen said, "I think I'd better. She's dead, Hans. She drowned last week."

Everybody made small shocked sounds except Frank Burch who snorted, and said, loudly and clearly, "Damn criminal shame, that's what it was!" Mrs. Henderson, apparently unruffled, asked, "If we're all rested enough, why don't we play some more?"

"Hans, you work for a while, I'll go put up some coffee," Owen said.

"Need any help?" Janice asked.

"Are you volunteering?"

"Sure."

"Okay, come on." They went out into the hall, and he led her toward the back of the house, through a dining room wallpapered in blue grasscloth, into an old-fashioned kitchen.

"What can I do?" she asked.

"Sit down and talk to me first, while I make the coffee. There's not much to do, we just put everything out on the table and let people help themselves." He ran water into the coffee pot. In the living room they began to play the Mozart Clarinet Quintet, and Owen whistled the theme while he measured coffee into the basket of the percolator. Janice sat at a white porcelain-topped kitchen table and watched. When he'd plugged in the pot, she said, "What's happened about Arlene, anyway?"

"What do you mean?" Owen continued to whistle softly as he took down cups and saucers and plates. "How many are we?" he asked, and they both counted. She picked up some of the cups and a box of paper napkins, and followed him into the dining room. "The silver's in there," he said, pointing to a drawer under one of the china cabinets. She took out spoons and knives, and set them out on the table. Caught up in the distant joyous sounds, she said, "I feel like a serving maid in a Mozart opera," and whirled around in time to the music.

"Do you?" Owen asked. "In that case I'll be delighted to play the Count," and he grabbed her as she pirouetted by, held her, and kissed her hard.

"La, sir!"

"Whee would be more like it," he remarked, and kissed her again. She broke out of his arms, turned away from him, and said, less to him than to herself, "All right, that's enough of that."

"What's the matter?"

"What exactly do you have in mind?"

He laughed. "The same thing you do."

"And after that?"

"I hadn't gotten quite that far yet. You travel fast."

"I have to be honest with you. I'm terrified of spending the rest of my life alone, living like I do now. I want a permanent relationship with somebody, preferably somebody wonderful. I'll bet that's not what you're thinking of at all."

"You might be right at that. Tell you what—"

"No thanks," she said, her arms folded and her back stiff.

"Boy, you sure have your guard up. You might at least let me finish."

"I've heard a lot of sentences that've begun, 'Tell you what'," she retorted, "and somehow they all end with the same verbs."

"You mean to tell me *every* man you meet asks you to go out to dinner with him?"

She blushed. "Your point," she said.

"Tomorrow night, then?"

"Love to. What time?"

"I'll pick you up about seven." He listened to the music. "Come on," he said, "let's get the rest of the things out, they're almost up to the second movement." He took cheeses out of the refrigerator, and while Janice arranged them on a wooden board, he filled baskets with crackers, and put out a plate of cookies. As they worked, Janice said, "You didn't answer about Arlene."

"No, I know I didn't."

"What've you found out?"

"Nothing definite."

"Was Roger responsible for her suicide?"

Owen looked unhappy.

"Well, yes, or no?"

"I can't tell you."

"Won't, you mean?"

"No. Can't." He jiggled the basket of crackers to make them lie flat and added some others on top. "This case makes me furious. Everything about it slips through my fingers except the facts that she was raped and she killed herself. I know it was Benton who attacked her. I know it, but I can't prove it. The evidence is entirely circumstantial, everybody else at the party had gone and left her with him and there's no witness to what must have happened. There's the medical evidence for the rape, but the only charge I could hope to get an indictment on, since she was past the age of consent, is for assaulting a girl of unsound mind. And I know that I wouldn't stand a chance of getting him convicted."

"Why not? She was mentally ill."

"Oh sure. Her doctor says so and so does her medical record. But both her parents swore to me there was nothing wrong with her. Why, they wouldn't even tell me the name of her psychiatrist or where she'd been hospitalized, and if her brother hadn't given me the information behind their backs, I'd still be trying to find

168

out. And you see, if Benton's lawyer got hold of them, which of course he would, and they came into court and denied in front of a jury that there was anything wrong with their daughter, there goes my case. There's sure to be at least one person on the jury who'll take their word against all the psychiatrists in the world, somebody who has his own reasons for denying insanity or who hates doctors or who's sentimental about motherhood or some other fool reason. And he gets off scot free." He jammed his hands in his pockets and glared at her.

"What about the brother, wouldn't he testify for you?"

"It wouldn't mean much if his parents contradicted his statements. Besides, he's so paralyzed himself I doubt if I could even get him to go on the stand. When I asked him in front of his mother if he knew who Arlene's doctor was, he wouldn't answer at all. The only way he could tell me was to write it on a slip of paper and find somebody to smuggle it to me, luckily, as it happened, Dave Haller. So that's where it stands—nowhere."

And that's where it stayed as far as Owen was concerned. Except that two days later Martin came into the police station—marched in would be more like it—and asked Owen pointblank when he was going to arrest Roger.

"On what charge?" Owen wanted to know.

"How do I know, I'm not a policeman. Assault—rape—murder."

"Whose?"

"Arlene's."

"Who told you he raped Arlene?"

"Isn't it true?"

"I can't answer that."

"Why not? I pay taxes in this town, don't forget. I'm

169

entitled to know what's going on.''

"Nobody is entitled to make that kind of serious accusation about anyone unless he can prove it. Do you have any real evidence that Benton assaulted her?''

Martin just stared at him.

"No? Then for your own sake, as well as for his, I strongly advise you not to go around making statements like that in public.''

"I don't need advice, Owen, I need action. Is he going to be punished for this crime or not?''

"Crimes against morality aren't my job unless they're also crimes against the law. I've done everything I could in this case, but I have to work within the law, Martin. Which means I can't always do what's wanted or what's needed or what's right, just what's possible.''

"I see. So I can't count on you, either.''

"What?'' He'd spoken so indistinctly that Owen wasn't able to make out the words.

"Never mind.'' Martin turned away.

"Just one minute. Why are you so concerned with Benton?''

"You wouldn't understand why. It's a question of morality.'' With which he marched himself out of the police station, leaving Owen to brood.

18

The first inkling Miranda had that there was anything wrong with the car came far too late for her to be able to do much about it. She'd left the relatively level part of the road, so she'd already missed the chance to save herself by steering off into a meadow. And because she was in such a hurry, she took the first part without braking

170

at all, and was already traveling too fast when the car nosed down into the steep and forested part of the road. She put her toe on the brake to slow down on the first hairpin curve, but instead of opposing its expected resistance, the pedal surrendered beneath her pressure with a heartsickening ease, and her foot went all the way to the floorboard without checking the speed of the car in the slightest. She immediately reached for the handle of the emergency brake and pulled it up all the way. It followed her hand obediently enough, but as far as affecting her speed, she might as well not have bothered. Nothing happened except that, because she was steering with one hand, the car slewed in the stony ruts and almost went out of control. And, of course, she picked up a little velocity. Fatally unable to consider any course of action except the one of mastering events—if she'd let the car run off into the ditch even then she might have survived the impact—she wasted precious seconds fighting it back on to the road. As soon as she could, she pushed the gear shift lever into first, then into low. With a grinding wrench that nearly jerked her head off her neck, the car slowed. But it didn't stop, and her last hope of controlling it was gone. The grade was very steep now, and despite the drag of the low gear the automobile was gaining momentum. It occurred to her then that she might jump out, but one look at the rocks in the roadbed and she discarded the idea. She'd left herself no choice but to ride to the bottom of the mountain and hope for the best. She gripped the steering wheel with all her strength and leaned one elbow on the horn. The car hurtled along in an ever swifter and seemingly endless descent. The tree trunks blurred, then merged into a solid and menacing wall. Pine branches whipped first at the windows on one side and then on the other as the car swayed more and more dangerously, caroming on the curves from the edge of one side ditch to the other. Her constantly accelerating progress, the blaring screech of the horn, the rising whine of the motor stopped only when the gears, strained beyond all conceivable tolerance, finally stripped. The car skidded off the road, almost but not quite vaulted the ditch, turned over, and rolled itself and her into the unyielding embrace of the trees.

19

Owen followed Horace's car up the hill. Martin was sitting in the middle of the road, keeping a vigil, waiting for them. Once they got Miranda's body out from underneath the car and into the ambulance, they went up to the house and Owen heard what Horace and Martin had to say.

"We were coming up the hill when we found her," Horace said, his voice shaking.

"How come you two were together?"

"I was taking a walk after breakfast," Martin explained, "and I ran into Horace. He said he was about to go to the village and did I want to ride with him. It saved me a trip, so I said yes."

"How long were you in Leesfield?"

"About an hour or so. I went to the post office and the liquor store, picked up a copy of the *Times*, and came back to the car. Martin came to the post office with me, and then said he was going to the supermarket."

"That's right. When I got out, Horace was waiting for me in the parking lot."

"Where was Miranda going?"

"I have no idea. She was heading for the office when

172

I left. Only reason she'd have to go to Leesfield would be to pick up the mail, and she knew I was already doing it."

Owen found Roger in his cabin, typing.

"Again? What is it this time? Make it quick, I'm working."

"Brace yourself, Benton. Miranda's had an accident."

"You're kidding. What happened?"

"She was driving your car."

"My car? How bad is it?"

"She's dead."

"Dead? My God. What about the car?"

"Totaled."

Roger stared at him, stunned. "What was she doing in my car? Where was she going?"

"I hoped you could tell me that."

"I don't know. I didn't even know she'd taken it."

"Where was it?"

"In that shed behind her house. It's the only covered garage space available, and I hate to leave it out all the time. I can't believe what you're telling me."

"Where were the keys?"

"Mine are right here." He picked them up off the desk. "Mandy kept an extra set just in case she ever needed wheels in a hurry."

"You let her drive it?"

"Let her? Are you joking? Mandy's a fantastic driver, better than practically anybody else I know. Of course I let her drive it."

"Was there anything wrong with it?"

"Not that I know of. I had it in the garage, Ed Phillip's place, last week for a tune up. Perfect condition." He buried his head in his hands. "Poor Mandy."

"How's Horace taking it?" Janice asked.

"Well of course he's devastated," Cathleen said. "I wanted to stay at the house with him, but he said no, he'd go to bed right away, and if he couldn't sleep he'd come and get me. He seems all right. I wouldn't have left him if he didn't."

"He probably hasn't felt the real impact of it yet."

"I think that's true. I bet it'll hit him hard in a couple of days. It must've been ghastly for him, finding her like that. It's really spooky that nobody seems to know why she was going down to Leesfield, if that's where she *was* going. You'd think if anybody did know where she was taking his car, it would be Roger. And he says he has no idea."

Janice put her cup down and looked at her watch. "It's past one."

"More tea?"

"No thanks, I've had plenty."

Flosshilde, who was lying on the floor in front of Cathleen's bed, raised her head and growled a little in the back of her throat. "Stop that," Cathleen ordered. "You know how I hate a nervous dog." Woglinda, who was asleep, opened her eyes, blinked, and in one quick move heaved herself up on her haunches. She whined and Flosshilde whined back.

"What do you think they hear?"

"Just a rabbit, probably." Cathleen registered careless bravado but not quite convincingly enough.

The dogs looked at one another and made a decision. They both walked stifflegged toward the door.

"Honestly, I don't know why we're all so jumpy tonight. It must be a reaction to this afternoon." Cathleen went over to the door and opened it. The dogs paced forward a trifle and stood looking warily into the long, almost pitchblack hall, their ears pricked and their uncropped tails tucked down between their legs.

"Well, I—goodnight, Cathleen."

"Do you want Flosshilde to sleep in your room?"

Janice hesitated, then shook her head. "Why are we frightening ourselves like this? It's ridiculous. See you tomorrow." And she advanced determinedly out the door.

"Wait, we'll walk you down the hall."

"Cathleen, please, all you're doing is scaring both of us to death." Nonetheless she was comforted to hear the click of the dogs' nails on the bare wood floor behind her. The four of them moved out of the light. Halfway down the corridor Cathleen gripped Janice's arm. Janice stifled a scream and a jump. "Don't do that!" she started to say, but Cathleen put her finger to her lips and whispered, "Somebody's trying to get in downstairs."

Janice listened as well as she could for the blood pounding in her ears. She identified the muffled snap of the curled spring latch being eased into place by a careful hand, then furtive steps shuffling across the stone floor toward the stairs that led to their rooms. Cathleen held Flosshilde's collar tight. With her other hand she hit Woglinda lightly across the rump. "Go see who that is," she whispered, and the dog was off like a shot in full deep bark.

"Oh Christ," a man's voice said, and a flashlight shone in Woglinda's face as she launched herself off the top step. "Get down!"

"It's Ezra!" Janice ran to the head of the stairs, Cathleen behind her. Flosshilde nearly knocked both of them over as she passed, trying to get there in time to be in on the kill.

"Down, down," Cathleen ordered, and the dogs, who were jumping up to lick Ezra's face, finally subsided.

"I'm sorry. I didn't want to wake you, that's why I

175

tried to sneak in," Ezra explained. "I forgot about the dogs."

"Next time don't be so thoughtful and just wake us. It'll be less of a strain," Cathleen advised him. "What do you want, anyway?"

"I have to make a phone call."

"But why not use the phone in the dorm? or in the main house?"

"I didn't want to."

"Who do you have to talk to at this hour? Is there something else wrong?"

"I can see," Ezra said, "that I'd've had more privacy practically anywhere else."

"Well, you owe us something for scaring us half to death," Janice pointed out. "If there's something going on, we want to know what it is, that's all."

"I am about to call Owen," he informed her. "Will that pay my debt to you?"

"Why?"

"Go away." He turned his back on them, took the receiver off the hook, and deposited a dime.

"Don't you want some light?" Cathleen asked.

"No! Hello, operator, I want to talk to Owen Henderson, I don't know his phone number, but I'm a physician, and this is an emergency, would you please ring him at home? Hello, Owen—Ezra. Sorry to get you out of bed like this but I think—look, I can't explain right now, but would you drive up here and meet me at Roger's cabin? Yes, now. I'll tell you why when I see you. As soon as you can. Right." And he hung up.

"What is it, what's happened?"

"I don't know that anything's happened. I'm afraid something might, that's all."

"To Roger?"

"To Roger."

"What?"

176

"I can't tell you because I don't know." He bowed. "Good night, ladies."

"I'm coming with you," Janice stated.

"No, you're not."

"Yes I am. If you won't wait for me, I'll follow you up the hill."

"Janice, please. There's probably nothing wrong, I'm simply imagining things. Now go to bed like a good girl."

"No."

"Me too," Cathleen said. "We can take the dogs."

"Oh, all right," Ezra said, "goddam it, all right. I know when I'm licked."

"I'll get a flash and sweater, and be right down," Cathleen said.

"What is it?" Janice asked. "What do you think you're imagining?"

"Do you remember that day when it was raining and we were in the potting shed talking about salon analysis?"

"Yes."

"And I said I tried very hard to keep my conclusions unconscious?"

"Yes."

"Well, one conclusion I'd managed to repress finally percolated through to me. Miranda came in that afternoon—"

Cathleen came running down the stairs carrying two flashlights and sweaters. "I'll tell you later," Ezra said.

The moon was full, and bright enough so that they hardly had to use their lights. Flanked by the dogs they walked up the hill, keeping well to the middle of the road, and not saying a word. The main house was dark as they passed. So was Roger's cabin. Ezra tapped on the door and called softly, "Roger. Roger." There was no answer. Woglinda sniffed, then whined and scratched at the door, looking up at Ezra as though to ask if she were being helpful. He patted her head, and called again, "Roger! Are you in there?" No answer.

He put his hand on the knob, and then, with an exclamation, took it away and held it so that the moonlight fell on the dark stain across his palm. He automatically closed his hand and touched the tips of his fingers to it, testing its consistency. Very carefully and slowly then he twisted the knob and pushed the door open so that it lay flat against the wall on his right. Without moving from the doorstep, he switched on his flashlight and moved the beam all around the room, shining it into the corners to make sure nobody was hiding there. Then he reached inside and flipped on the overhead light.

"Roger!" Janice cried. Ezra barred her entrance with his arm. "Let me check first!" He ran to kneel over the body huddled in the middle of the floor. Disregarding his order, both women were right beside him.

Roger lay on his back, his body oozing blood out of a couple of dozen stab wounds, some of them deep, some of them superficial. His hands already busy, Ezra's mind rapidly estimated the medical emergency presented by the man in front of him whose life was ebbing away with every sticky drop.

"Cathleen," he ordered, "go to my room in the dorm, it's on the second floor, right off the stairs, my card's on the door, you can't miss it. My bag's in the closet, right in front, on the floor. Get up there as fast as you can, and get it and bring it back here. Take one of the dogs with you, don't stop to talk to anybody, hear me? and get back here as fast as you can."

Without a word Cathleen ran out, taking Flosshilde with her.

"Now, you," he said to Janice. "Take the other dog and get down to the main house and wake Horace, and

178

tell him to move his ass up here as fast as he can and no excuses. Tell him Roger's hurt. If he asks you if he's dead, tell him you don't know. Then you call—don't let him do it—*you* call Owen and make sure that he gets on his way immediately if he hasn't already left."

"Is he—will you be able to—"

"Don't bother me with questions, I'm busy. Get going and be sure to do exactly what I told you to. And," he called after her, "don't you dare go outside that house again alone."

She flew down the hill, the dog scampering beside her, cut across the lawn, and threw open the front door so violently that it slammed against the wall. Switching on the hall light, she ran up the front stairs. "Horace," she called, "Horace! Wake up, wake up!" Nobody answered, and she pounded on the door of their bedroom and pushed it open. She walked into the room groping for the string to the overhead bulb. After a small eternity, she found it and pulled. The bed was empty, although it had been slept in. "Horace, where are you?" She ran out into the hall, and by shining her flashlight into the bedrooms on the second floor found out that they were all unoccupied. She finally ended up standing on the dim landing, unable to make up her mind what to do. "Horace!" she made one final attempt. "Where are you?"

"Right behind you."

She gasped and whirled. Horace stood in the doorway to the back staircase, fully dressed. "What do you want this time of night?"

"It's Roger, we just found him, he's—"

"Who's we?"

"Ezra and Cathleen and me."

"What do you mean, found him? Was he lost?"

"Somebody's stabbed him! Ezra wants you to come to his cabin. Right away."

179

"How bad is he hurt? Is he dead?"

"Oh, I don't know. Please, what difference does it make? Hurry!"

"All right, I'm going." He walked past her and down the front stairs. "You stay here. Don't go outside."

"No, I won't." The dog ran down the narrow staircase. Horace held the screen open and whistled. Woglinda, her ears up, trotted past him and out.

"Hey! Bring her back."

"You'll be all right. Just stay inside." Horace was gone. Janice did her best to fight down the unreasoning panic about being entirely alone in the house.

Then she remembered that Ezra had told her to call Owen, and ran into the office. The operator connected her, and Mrs. Henderson's voice said, "Hello?"

"This is Janice Hoskins up at Roundmount, Mrs. Henderson."

"Are you calling Owen?"

"Yes. Could I speak to him, please?"

"You just missed him, he left the house about two minutes ago. He should be up there in a little while. Is there anything I can do?"

"No thanks, I was calling him to ask him to hurry, but if he's already on his way, there's no need for that, is there?"

"Well, no, I guess not." When Janice didn't say anything more, she asked, "Are you all right?"

"Yes, thank you." Janice answered, gripping the phone as tight as she could. She wanted very much to say, No, no, I'm not, please don't hang up, I'm alone here in the house, and I'm terribly scared of something, I don't know what. But of course, she didn't.

"Well, then—"

"Good night, Mrs. Henderson, thank you." She put the phone back on the cradle, all excuse gone, and looked around the small room, lit too brightly by the naked hanging bulb. It was filled with Miranda's life: her reminders to herself on the desk calendar, pencils in one of her pots, her cigarettes, the folders neatly labeled in her firm handwriting. "Oh, I can't stay in *here*," Janice said aloud, and opened the door to the hall. She lit her way into the living room with her flashlight, switched on every single lamp in the room, and ground her back into the useless protection of a wingchair. She tried as hard as she could to read a magazine, but wasn't terribly successful because the memory of Roger's bleeding body kept coming between her and the print. She was staring blindly at the page when she heard the back screen door close, and quiet steps cross the kitchen floor. She sprang to her feet and the magazine slid off her lap onto the rug. "Who—who is it?" she said, her voice breaking like an adolescent boy's. "Who's there? Answer me!"

A man's voice said, "It's all right, it's only me, Martin." She heard a small rattling noise as though something wooden were being fitted into a socket, and a kitchen drawer opened and closed. "I saw the lights on and I came in to return something I'd borrowed."

"But it's two o'clock in the morning!"

"Is it that late? I didn't realize." He appeared in the doorway. "What're you doing here? are you alone?"

"I—yes." She sank back into the chair and he sat down opposite her on the sofa.

"But where's Horace?"

"He had to go out." Although she was thinking of nothing else, for some reason Janice didn't want to tell Martin about Roger. "I suppose you've heard about Miranda," she said instead.

"Why of course. You know I was with Horace when—when we found her."

"Yes, that's right, I did know. I'm sorry. I guess I'm not really myself tonight."

"After all that's happened in the last couple of weeks here—" His voice trailed off, and each of them retreated into private thought. Janice noticed, without thinking about it, that Martin's hair was wet, as if he'd just gotten out of a shower. Then she heard the faint whine of a car coming up the hill. She went to the window. The noise got louder, though too slowly to suit her, and only when she saw the beams from Owen's headlights and the flasher on top of the car did some of her tension dissipate in a sigh of relief.

Martin had walked over to the window and stood in back of her, peering out over her shoulder. "What're you looking for, Sister Anne?" he asked cheerfully.

"Owen. Owen's coming, that's his car." She turned around. Martin caught at her wrist. "Owen? Why's he coming here?"

"To take Roger—"

"Where?"

"Martin, let me go, I have to see if I can help."

"Help? Help who?"

"Roger."

"Why should you want to help Roger?" He grabbed her shoulder with his other hand and shook her.

"He's been stabbed. Somebody stabbed him."

"Isn't he dead?"

"No, no—" Wincing, she tried to get free of his grip. "Martin, let me go, I've got to get out there—oh, now look what you've done, you've made me miss them. It's too late."

The car had rushed past up the hill.

"So you want to help Roger, do you?"

"Of course, he needs—" She looked up at his face, and realized that he knew what had been done to Roger. "You—" she whispered. "You're the one—"

"Do you know what kind of a person Roger was?" His breath was warm on her cheek. "The kind of things

182

he did?"

"Let me go. I—"

"The awful things he did to girls? the way he forced himself on them like an animal, driving them to suicide, hurting them? And you still want to help him?"

"Martin—" She summoned the strength to try to break past him, but he gripped her wrist even tighter and stepped behind her, wrenching her arm around behind her back, twisting it up so that she bent over against him helpless with pain. She started to scream, but he clapped his other hand on her mouth, dragged her over to the couch, and flung her, face down, into the cushions. Gasping, shocked and stunned by his attack, half-suffocated, she lifted her head from the down pillows and opened her mouth to breathe. At once he crammed most of his handkerchief into it and tied the ends around her head; leaning his weight on her back so that she was unable to move, he pulled her blouse out of her slacks, tore off a piece of fabric, and bound her wrists tightly together behind her. He moved off her on to the couch, and she wriggled her body over, fighting to spit out the gag, to twist her arms free.

"That's the sort of thing Roger would do, it's the way he handles women, isn't it?" He was panting, his face suffused with blood. "Is this the way he treated you when he made love to you? when he raped you?"

Janice shook her head.

"Don't lie to me! Everybody thinks they can lie to me about that, even Mandy. First she betrayed me with him, and then she lied about it. And he made love to you too, just like he did to her, didn't he?" He tugged half her body upright and shook her so violently she thought her neck would snap in two. "But now she's dead, isn't she? *Isn't* she?" Janice managed to nod. "That's right." He let her drop back. "They're both dead. Oh, poor Mandy!" He put his face in his hands.

"He sent her out in his car, I know it. Sent her out to die like that. His fault." He raised his head. "It makes a pattern, doesn't it? He raped Arlene and she died. He raped Miranda and she died. And if he raped you, I suppose you have to die too."

Janice shrieked a strangled no! into the gag.

"And Roger's dead, I know he's dead. You only told me he was alive to tease me. He couldn't be. I made too many holes in him, like he made holes in Arlene, where her life ran out to the turtles to eat. I know I killed him like he killed her."

He cocked his head. "That sound's a car door closing. Owen'll be coming back soon. I suppose I have to get you out of here. Let me see. It's too bright out to take you up to my house by the main road, even after they've all left. And it's too risky to take you up by the back path. You might be able to get away from me. I can't tie your ankles, and you're too big to carry. I guess—yes, I guess the potting shed's the nearest place."

He pulled her up off the couch and propped her up on her feet. She sagged against him and slipped heavily to the floor. "Oh, no, you don't," he said, and twined his hand in her hair and tugged hard. "Upsydaisy." She resisted, despite the pain. "If you don't get up," he threatened, "I'll have to kill you right here this second. It doesn't matter to me."

She scrambled clumsily to her feet, and he steered her ahead of him into the kitchen, one hand on her manacled wrists and the other gripping the nape of her neck. "Hold it," he said, "I need my equipment again." He reached his left hand up to the wooden rack and picked out a long, thin-bladed knife.

"Let's go," he ordered. "You know the way." She heard the car again, headed down the hill. "Here they come, hurry up." He shoved her out the door, across

184

the porch, down the steps. The car didn't slow up as it passed the house. "I guess they're more worried about Roger than they are about you," Martin said, and laughed as he pushed her along.

Outside Roger's cabin the four of them watched Mike drive away with Roger's still, but barely, living flesh.

"Now," Owen said, "let's start with you, Horace."

"Me? I don't know anything about this. The first I heard of it was when Janice came running into the house to tell me."

"How did she know?"

"She was with Cathleen and me," Ezra explained. "I sent her down for him."

"Where is she now?"

"I hope still in the house. I warned her not to go out alone."

"She shouldn't be there by herself."

"Woglinda's with her," Cathleen told him. "She'll be safe enough."

"No—look!" Ezra pointed at both dogs sniffing around Roger's doorstep.

Owen began running down the hill. The others raced to catch up, but only the dogs got ahead of him. The main house was lit up downstairs, so that Owen was able to see there was no one in the living room. He pushed the front door open, and yelled "Janice! Are you in the house?" When there was no answer, he took his gun out and stepped warily into the hall. "Answer me!" Silence. He went up the stairs two at a time, and explored the rooms on the second floor. They were deserted. He could hear Ezra and Cathleen searching through the rooms below him, calling for Janice, and he ran down to join them.

Ezra said, "Owen, I think—"

"Quiet! Did you hear that?"

"What?"

"Come on!" He sprinted through the kitchen, and out the back door.

Janice stumbled and dragged her feet as much as she could on the path, but all too soon Martin was unlatching the shed door. "In you go," he said, and pushed. She lost her balance, tripped, and sprawled full length on the cold cement floor. He came after her in the darkness that, gravelike, smelled of wet clay and mold. She struggled to get up, but her bound wrists hampered her, and he pounced on her and knocked her flat before she had done more than get to her knees. He crouched at her side, silhouetted against the square of paleness framed by the open door, and raised his arm. The blade poised over his head caught the moonlight. Instinctively she jacknifed her torso away from the descending weapon, and with the same convulsive movement kicked out at his bent legs with both her feet. He grunted with pain and surprise, and the knife came down on the floor an eighth of an inch away from her cringing ribs. Sparks flew, and the top two inches of the narrow blade splintered off across the concrete.

Seizing her small advantage, she began to wriggle away from him, hitching and scraping her body along the floor toward whatever protection she might be able to find among the chairs and tables. He stalked after her, heading her away from the furniture. As soon as he got within range, she kicked out at his shins again. He stepped back, bumped into one of the chairs, knocked it over, picked it up, and shied it at her. The edge of its seat bounced off her shoulder; the chair rolled away, and banged into the metal drip pan under the sink. He drove her in front of him by threatening her with wild swings of the knife until he'd made her travel all the way back across the floor to the open space near the door.

When she was in the clear he laughed and said, "All right, now!" and sprang, falling across her and pinning her hopelessly underneath him. He mounted astride her body, his knees digging into her breasts, his buttocks on her stomach. She bucked and twisted as hard as she could, but knew she would never dislodge him. He held her head against the floor, spreading the palm of his free hand over her nose and mouth, then slid the heel of his hand under her chin and levered her face up to one side, grinding her cheek into the cement and exposing the length of her throat. Strangled and suffocated, bruised, shocked, Janice had reached the limit of her stength. She stayed conscious only long enough to see, out of the corner of one wildly straining eye, that he was ready to strike again. Her final thought, as blackness washed over her brain, was one of amazement at learning that when a knife was pushed inside your body to murder you, it made the same kind of noise as a gun going off.

20

"The ambulance'll be here as soon as they can get up the hill," Cathleen reported. "How is she?"

"She'll be all right," Ezra replied. "He nicked her shoulder, but it's not serious. It's mainly shock."

"Here's blankets." Horace came into the shed with an armful.

"Thanks." Very carefully Ezra tucked them around the two unconscious figures. He knelt by Martin's body, taking his pulse, listening to the way he was breathing. "Where's Owen?"

"Still on the phone. Here." He handed a flask to Cathleen. "Brandy. We all need it."

She took a swallow, then passed it to Ezra. "The alcohol'll kill the germs."

He drank and gave the flask back to Horace, who took a long pull.

"How are they?" Owen asked as he walked in.

"She's okay. I'm not so sure about him."

"I called Northampton, a neurosurgeon who's on the staff there is on his way. It shouldn't take him long, he's got a police escort and the roads're empty."

"Why bother?" Horace said. "He'll only have to spend the rest of his life in jail. Might as well save the state a little money."

"Horace!" Even Cathleen was shocked.

He stared at them all defiantly, then turned his face away. "It's been kind of a rough day for me, you know." Cathleen immediately went over and put her arm around his shoulder.

Martin's eyelids twitched and he groaned. "Don't try to move," Ezra ordered softly. "You'll be all right in a little while."

"Whuh—uh—" His eyes opened and stared blindly up at the ceiling.

"Lie quiet," Ezra insisted.

"Mandy—not you—"

Owen knelt beside Ezra. "Martin, can you talk?"

Martin gradually focused his gaze. "Head hurts," he whispered.

Ezra restrained his arm. "Don't move. Owen, can't you do this later on, he's in no condition—"

Martin closed his eyes and opened them again. "Kill Roger." His voice got a little stronger. "Have to. Nobody else. Bad." His eyes slipped up in his head, the lids only half-closed so that white slits showed between his lashes.

"All right, that's enough!" Ezra said angrily. "Unless you want to finish him off altogether."

"What did you want me to do, try something fancy like shooting the knife out of his hand in the moonlight instead of aiming at his head?" Owen snarled, and heaved himself erect. "Or stand there and see him kill her?"

"There's the ambulance," Cathleen said.

Owen went out and came back with two uniformed men. He and Ezra helped them transfer Janice and Martin on to stretchers, and then into the ambulance. The rest of the students had gathered in the road, watching silently.

Two police cars pulled up. Mike got out of the first and a state trooper out of the second. "Now what?" Mike asked. The ambulance driver snicked the latch shut on the back ambulance door. "This place is getting to be like a regular stop on a bus route," he said.

"Very funny," Owen snapped. "Get going." The driver shrugged. "How's Benton?"

"They were giving him transfusions when I left. Dr. Burch's there."

"Are you going to the hospital?" Ezra asked.

"After a while."

"I'll ride down with you, all right? There may be something I can do."

"Okay." Owen took the trooper aside and spoke to him in a low voice, then came back to Horace. "I'll be here in the morning. I'm leaving a man on guard." He turned to Ezra and Mike. "Come on," he said, and led them toward the car. "Mike, I want you to stay at Martin's cabin. I'll send someone to relieve you as soon as I can. Don't let anybody in."

At Martin's house Owen and Mike went in. Ezra could see them moving around inside, then Owen came back to the car.

"What made you call me and go looking for Roger?" he asked Ezra.

"I was just about to fall asleep when I remembered that the other day Miranda had come to the potting shed looking for one of her kitchen knives she said was missing. And then my mind jumped to Martin. I'd run into him on the road last night when I was on my way to the art shed after dinner. He looked so scruffy I asked him if he was growing a beard, but instead of answering he mumbled something about, 'Roger did it. I know he did.' And then he said something about punishment I didn't catch. I said, 'What?' but he didn't answer, just turned and walked away. I meant to talk to Mandy about him, but I didn't see her this morning, and then of course the accident put it completely out of my head. Until, as I say, I remembered about the knife and made some kind of connection with Martin, I don't know why. I tried to tell myself I was over-interpreting, but the more I thought about it, the uneasier I felt. Till eventually I got up and called you. I suppose maybe I should have called you right away, last night after I saw him, but I guess that's hindsight."

"I already knew about it. Martin came into the station yesterday and asked me what I intended to do about Arlene's death." Owen sighed. "I told him the truth, that there was nothing I could do. I thought about warning Roger, but I figured he'd only use it to make more trouble."

"Yes. Taken it as a challenge and found some way to brace Martin about it in front of other people and humiliate him."

"Besides, you know, Martin didn't make any overt threat against Roger. And if he had accused Roger in front of other people, Roger would simply use whatever he said to support his position that nobody can *prove* he had anything to do with Arlene's suicide."

From a long way off Janice heard voices. She opened her eyes. Ezra was standing there talking to a woman in a white dress. They looked very small and dim, as though they were a mile away at the end of a long tunnel. "Hi," she said, and drifted out. When she came back, she could see Ezra clearly and life-sized.

"You're out of the tunnel," she said.

"So are you." He came up to the bed and took her hand. "How do you feel?"

"Funny. Where is this?"

"You're in the hospital. You're okay. Your face and shoulder will be sore for a couple of days, but other than that you have nothing to worry about."

She remembered. "Oh, Christ, Ezra, Martin was—he was killing me."

"Owen stopped him in time. You're not killed."

"Nice to know." She closed her eyes again, and the next time she woke up it was for good. When Owen came in that afternoon she was sitting up in a chair.

"You look swell," he said.

"I feel all right. I understand I owe you my life. Thank you."

"Think nothing of it. Do you feel able to talk about it? I've got someone here to take down a statement."

"I think so." After she'd answered all his questions and the stenographer had left, she asked, "And what happened then?"

"I got there just when you fainted and shot him."

"Oh. Is he—?"

"Still alive. More or less. He's in critical condition."

"And Roger?"

"He's here, too. I just talked to him."

"Martin was the one who stabbed him?"

"Yes, he told you the truth. Roger's story is that he was up late writing, and Martin knocked on the door. When Benton opened it, he just jumped on him like a maniac without saying a word. Roger must've been so taken by surprise that he never had a chance to fight back. He'll be in the hospital for a couple of weeks, and

191

when he does get out he's going to have several new dimples in a number of unlikely places."

"It's hard to feel sorry for him, somehow. But I'm glad he'll get better."

"The doctor tells me you can be discharged tomorrow. I want you to stay in town, please, for a few more days."

"I only want to be here long enough to leave, thank you very much. I can't face the idea of staying at Roundmount for one more night. I'm not even sure I can bring myself to go up there to pack."

"That's okay. You can stay with us, how about that?"

"I couldn't. That would be imposing."

"Not at all, my mother will be delighted to have you. Aren't you even a little bit interested to see how all this is going to come out?"

"What do you mean, all this?"

"You city kids are sure blasé. One rape, one suicide, one probable murder, and two assaults with a deadly weapon, and they don't even seem to pique your curiosity."

"Probable murder? Who?"

"Miranda."

"You're kidding." She looked at his face. "You're not kidding. Who did it?"

"I'm not ready to say yet." He got up. "I have to go out of town this afternoon for a day or so. Someone will pick you up and take you over to the house. I've already asked Cathleen to pack your stuff and bring it down for you." He bent over and kissed her lightly. "See you when I come back."

21

The day Owen got back to Leesfield, he asked Janice to come with him to his office in the afternoon. When they walked in, Cathleen, Horace, Ezra, and Dave were already sitting there, talking to Mike.

"I'm taping this conversation," Owen announced, and pushed the record button on a cassette machine set up on a stand next to his desk.

"Why?" Dave wanted to know.

"It will be useful for me. Anyone who wants a transcript can have one."

"Is this some kind of official meeting, then?" Ezra asked.

"Yes." He paused. "I think we've finally come to the end of this string of disasters. And since you've all been more or less involved, I think you should know why and how they happened."

"Are you saying that they're somehow related?" Dave asked.

"Yes, I am."

"But surely each one of them was a separate event? Done for different personal reasons, not for any one cause?"

"That's partly true, Ezra, but it's not the whole story. Maybe the best way to describe this summer is to say it was a series of not entirely random coincidences."

"That doesn't make sense. Either you have cause and effect, or you don't."

"You'll see what I mean."

"Besides, Ezra," Cathleen argued, "some of them are related. Martin's responsible for what happened to both Roger and Janice."

"But for different reasons," Janice pointed out. "He hated Roger, okay, and thought he was avenging Arlene when he stabbed him. That part's fairly clear, however bizarre. But in a sense it was a kind of accident, almost a spinoff from the main event. That's being a lot fairer to him than I really want to be, but it's true. He didn't plan to kill me. When he came into the house he had absolutely no idea he'd find me there, how could he? or that we'd end up on the potting shed floor together."

"And Mandy's death was accidental," Dave said. "So that's three things that aren't related."

"Mandy's death wasn't an accident. It was murder."

"That's news to me," Horace said. "And I can't say I care for being told about it in this offhanded way, either."

"Sorry, Horace, but I just found out about it for sure myself. The car's been checked by experts at the state lab. They are certain its brakes were destroyed before it crashed."

"That's ridiculous. How could they say that? It was a complete and total wreck. I saw it."

"Believe me, they're sure. The brakes had been tampered with before Mandy started to drive that car."

"But wouldn't she notice that when she drove it out on to the road from the driveway?" Janice asked. "Didn't she have to stop to turn around?"

"Good point. Because there is something strange here. Roger wasn't going to use the car for a few days, that's why he parked it inside. And he swears that when he drove the car into the shed, he did not back in. That is, the car was facing the back of the shed. But I have a witness who saw Mandy drive the car out of the garage, and he testifies that she came out of the shed already heading into the road."

"That's right," Dave said. "The witness is me. I was

on my way to the office to see Mandy, and I was crossing the side lawn just as she drove out of the shed. She was definitely not backing out. I yelled to her, but she didn't hear or else didn't pay any attention. She didn't even slow down at the end of the driveway, just turned left, gave it a lot of gas, and zoomed off." He shook his head. "Like the ads say, from zero to sixty in twenty-two seconds. And if she kept accelerating like that, which she probably did, she was going a lot faster than she should have been by the time she started down the steep part of the hill."

"Therefore," Owen said, "someone seems to have turned the car around so there'd be almost no reason, no chance to brake until it was too late to stop."

"But what about the keys?" Cathleen asked. "Nobody could move the car without the keys."

"Roger tells me Miranda had a spare set. Where did she keep them, Horace, do you know?"

"Have no idea. Maybe in her bag, maybe in the desk drawer. I've never touched Roger's car, so I had no reason to ask her where they were."

"I see. Ezra, let me ask you again for an expert opinion. Assuming he knew how to do it to begin with, do you think Martin could have managed that kind of mechanical job?"

"You mean, was he mentally able to concentrate on a time-consuming and complicated activity a day or so before he blew his top completely?" Ezra thought. "If you're willing again to take an educated guess, I'd say no, not in the shape he was in that evening when I saw him. Even if he knew how to do it, I think he was probably too far gone by then to be able to focus on any task that took time and patience. Wildly indiscriminate, explosive physical behavior, like stabbing Roger a dozen times, would be about his limit. Any kind of co-ordinated problem solving, most likely no. But of course I couldn't swear to that, one way or the other. A lot would depend on how familiar he is with machinery, whether he'd always done a lot of tinkering, or not."

Owen laughed. "Your usual noncommittal reply. When Martin's able to talk, I'll ask him."

"He'll deny he knew anything about it, won't he?" Horace said. "He's not that crazy."

"I'll find that out, too. In the meantime, did you ever notice anyone going into or out of the shed, or see the car being turned around?"

Horace shrugged. "There's a lot of traffic out there. People are always cutting across the back yard to see Mandy in the office. Roger drives his car in and out all the time. I wouldn't pay any attention to anyone I did see."

"Martin must have come that way when he walked in the back door," Janice said.

"He was in and out of the back yard all the time," Horace agreed. "Just like everybody else."

"That brings us to Arlene." Owen took a deep breath.

Cathleen asked, "Surely that was suicide? That had nothing to do with anybody but herself."

"Yes, it was suicide all right. Bear with me a minute, please, Horace, and tell me again how Arlene happened to be at Roundmount. I think you said her folks wrote in for a brochure?"

"I think I said that I didn't know how she got here for sure, but I assume that's what happened. When people answer the ad, Mandy takes—took care of the inquiries. She sent out application forms and took the deposits. I never had anything to do with it."

"But you did audition her?"

"Yes, in Chicago. I was there on business, so Mandy asked me to arrange to hear her play."

"No other contact with the family?"

"No."

Owen nodded. "Yes. That's what you told me before, all right. At least you're a consistent liar."

"Now wait a minute! What do you mean, I'm a liar?"

"Stop yelling, Horace, relax and sit down. I've got a tape to play for you." He took a cassette out of his drawer and put it in the machine. "You should find it interesting."

He pushed the play button. His own voice said, "This statement is being recorded in Chicago. The information herein is in reference to the death of Arlene Horowitz. What is your name, please?"

A flat New England voice said, "Clara Allen."

Horace stood up again. Owen turned off the cassette.

"What the hell is this? I don't have to sit here and listen to any tape. And I won't."

"Horace," Cathleen said. "Why are you going? Where?"

"It won't do you any good to walk out," Owen said. "This isn't some kind of contract negotiation where you try to bluff your way into better terms."

"I walk, buster. And you can't stop me."

He slammed the door behind him.

"Okay, Mike," Owen said. "Keep an eye on him. If he tries to leave town, let me know." Mike nodded and went out.

Cathleen said, "What is this? Why are you saying those things about him? What's he supposed to have done?"

"Among other things, killed his wife."

"What proof do you have?"

"His prints were on the key-holder and the keys to Roger's car, and all over the chassis. And as you all just heard him say, he claims he never touched it."

"Are you sure?"

"Cathleen, we have this new laser gadget at the state lab. It can probably take identifiable fingerprints off a slice of fresh bread, let alone an automobile. Don't ask me why he didn't wear gloves. Maybe he figured the car would burn when it crashed. Maybe it was just too awkward and he couldn't work properly in them. Maybe he didn't think anyone was going to look."

"But why would he want to kill Mandy?" Dave asked.

"He wasn't necessarily aiming at her. I think it didn't matter to him who was in that car, just so long as somebody crashed. Roger would have been just as good."

"But why? I don't believe Horace is so callous. You make him sound like a monster."

"What Horace has been doing this summer has been hard to see. But I know he did it, and I know why. And I'm absolutely certain that he'll be tried and convicted for doing it."

"What's on that tape?" Ezra asked.

"No harm in playing it for you." Owen ran it back, and started it over again. The voice once again said, "Clara Allen."

"Where do you live, Miss Allen?"

"Chicago."

"Are you employed?"

"Yes. I work for M. H. Textile Machines."

"Your position there?"

"Private secretary to Milton Horowitz, president of the company. I'm really his executive assistant."

"How long have you worked in that capacity?"

"Eight years."

"Did you know his daughter Arlene?"

"Of course. She was still a child when I came to work for her father. I've seen her in the office a lot, and in addition I've heard a great deal about her from her mother. Mrs. H. calls the office very frequently, sometimes five or six times a day. Mr. H. usually can't or won't take her calls, so I have to talk to her. I probably know as much about Arlene's life as Arlene did. Maybe more."

"Did you ever hear her play?"

"Yes, many times. I don't know much about music, but she seemed to be very good for her age. Lord knows they made enough of a fuss about her talent."

"What is your relationship to Miranda and Horace Boardman?"

"I'm Horace's first cousin. Our mothers were sisters."

"Are you friendly with them?"

"We don't see each other too often, but we keep in touch. They're family. I must say Miranda's accident came as quite a shock."

"I'm sure. When was the last time you saw her?"

"Oh, five, maybe six years ago."

"And Horace?"

"Sometime last April. I'd have to look in my book to be sure of the exact date."

"Why was he in Chicago, do you know?"

"Yes. He came to enroll Arlene at Roundmount."

"Will you please explain how that happened?"

"Well, since it's pretty plain now how batty Arlene was, I don't suppose there's any harm in telling you that they had to put her in an asylum for a while. She'd been behaving very strangely for a long time, and I guess it finally got to the point where they had no choice. Dr. Steiner suggested when she got out that they should send her to a music camp for the summer, it would do her good, which they agreed to do. Naturally I got stuck with the job of finding one for her, and of course I immediately thought of Roundmount. I called Horace and asked him if Roundmount wouldn't take her, did he know of any other place that would?''

"You explained the situation? That is, about her having been hospitalized?''

"Certainly. After all, in case Arlene caused them any trouble, which I told Horace she was almost certain to do, I didn't want him or Miranda to be able to say later on that I didn't warn them. So that was the very first thing I said to him. Horace, I said, I must tell you that this girl has her problems. Frankly, I said, she's just out of the booby hatch. So he knew what was wrong with her, and he can't say he didn't.''

"What did he say when you told him?''

"He laughed and said all really talented people were crazy and he was used to it. As a matter of fact, the nuttier she was, he said, the better he might like it. Mandy might have objections, but he knew she'd put up with a good deal if Arlene was talented enough so that it would be worth while for Roundmount to be able to say that she'd been there. But he said he couldn't do anything about talking Mandy into taking her unless he heard her play first. He explained to me that it was like peddling any client, you have to be able to believe in them yourself.

"I told him I could send him a tape, but he said no, he'd want to see her himself, and he'd come out to Chicago sometime soon. Well, Mr. H. isn't the kind of man who's about to wait for somebody else's sometime soon, so I told Horace he'd have to come to Chicago right away or I'd have to make other arrangements. He thought for a couple of seconds, and said, well, it seemed to him that from what I said she might be worth a special trip, and he could take a morning flight the next day and would that be okay? And of course I said yes, and that it was very nice of him to do it. So then I arranged an appointment with Mrs. H. at the house, and Arlene played for him. When he came over to the office he couldn't say enough nice things about her. 'She's perfect,' he said. 'I couldn't ask for anyone better.' He gave me an application form, which I typed up, then I made out a deposit check for Mr. H. to sign, and it was all settled between them right then and there."

"So Horace had no illusions about Arlene's condition?"

"None whatsoever. I don't see how he could have. I didn't mince any words, I assure you. I told him she was looney, that she ran away, that she was hard to get along with, that she was almost certain to make waves. But it seemed to me that the more I warned him, the more set he was to have her."

Owen switched off the cassette. Janice asked, "But why? If he knew she was so apt to be bad news, why did he want her at Roundmount so much? It doesn't make sense."

"It does if you realize that bad news was exactly what he was looking for. What Horace has been trying to do all summer is to make sure that he sends Roundmount right down the tubes. Everything he's done has been aimed at destroying it. That's why he came up here full time, so he could keep an eye on what was going on and make it worse."

Dave turned on Ezra. "Don't you ever accuse me again of being paranoid. I told you the vibes were bad up here this year, and that it was because of him."

Cathleen leaned forward. "Why should Horace want Roundmount to go under? That's foolish. Horace hates failure, he always has."

"Because it wouldn't be failure for him, it would be success. He'd get just what he wanted out of it. A New York real estate combine wants to build a fancy ski resort here, and they have to own Roundmount to do it. They need the top of the mountan, they need the land, they can use the buildings. But all that belonged to Mandy, not to Horace, and when they made their offer, she told them to go to hell, it wasn't for sale for any price. Horace was certain she'd never agree to sell if Roundmount was going. But if it got enough bad publicity so that nobody would want to come, or if the newspapers were continually printing stories about terrible things that happened there, if the police were known to be always investigating something or other there, then Roundmount would be finished, and then maybe he'd be able to convince Mandy that she should sell after all.

"And this isn't just speculation, Cathleen, so don't look at me like that. I've spoken to the firm that made the offer, and she did refuse to sell to them, although Horace seemed very willing. Furthermore, I also happen to know that yesterday Horace stopped in at the local real estate broker to tell him that the property is now on the market, and to start negotations with the guys in New York."

"That's revolting. Mandy isn't even buried yet."

"That's the least of it, Ezra. Think about what he did to Arlene. He hears about this talented girl, really not much more than a child. He learns she's crazy, she's unhappy, she's very vulnerable and fragile. He decides he can use her and arranges to move her here as though she were not a person, but some kind of an object, like a little wooden pawn in his chess game. He goes along with whatever her father wants to make sure he does get her to Roundmount, including building a special cabin for her, arranging to move her piano here from Chicago, agreeing to put her teacher up when he comes from New York. Whatever Mr. Horowitz asked, Horace was glad to do. Because once Arlene got here, he could almost be positive that something would go very wrong. For one thing, a talented, rich, impressionable girl would be irresistible to Roger. If he didn't move in on her, which he was almost certain to do, there'd be some other way to exploit her potential. Maybe she'd run away again, so there'd be stories in the papers. Maybe she'd attack somebody. Maybe she'd set something on fire. Who knows what he hoped she'd do?

"And at the very least if nothing did develop that Horace could blow up into bad publicity, he'd get first crack at handling someone who was, he told me himself, sure to become a star performer. As far as he was concerned, she was a no-lose proposition for him. So she might get hurt—tough. So she killed herself—too bad.

"I can't prove it till I'm able to talk to him, but I'm certain that somehow Horace was also behind Martin's attack on Roger. Martin hated Roger to begin with, and all Horace would have had to do is egg him on, probably using Roger's contribution to Arlene's suicide to push him over the edge. As far as Mandy's death is concerned, I think he may have decided that he wasn't getting results fast enough by manipulating other people and so he decided to take a hand directly. Someone at the paper store saw Horace make a phone call that morning. The phone company records show that someone called Mandy's office number from that phone at about the same time that Horace was calling. My guess is that he called and told her something that he knew would make her take Roger's car and be in such a tearing hurry to get to the village she'd be driving too fast."

"But he couldn't be sure she'd kill herself," Ezra pointed out.

"That's true. But even if she hadn't, it would have meant another police investigation, more bad feelings, more gossip in Leesfield, another bad experience for the kids to write home about. As it turned out, Mandy did die, which he must have figured solved all his problems for him at once."

"What happens now?" Dave asked.

"I'll have a warrant for his arrest in a few hours. After that it will be in the courts."

Driving back to the house, Janice said, "When did you start to realize all this?"

"When Horace very carefully didn't tell me about his cousin Clara, after Miranda had mentioned her. Naturally it made me curious. So remember that. Never lie to me."

"Never?"

"At least not for the next fifty years."

THE CLAIRVOYANT
By Hans Holzer

PRICE: $2.25 T51573
CATEGORY: Novel (Hardcover publisher:
Mason/Charter 1976)

The story of a beautiful young Viennese girl whose
gift of prophecy took her from the mountains of
Austria to the glittering drawing rooms of Beverly
Hills. She began to exhibit psychic powers at the
age of four. Terrified of their daughter's "gift," her
parents sent her to a remote school. As she moved
from school to school and then from man to man,
she used her psychic abilities to climb to perilous
heights of fame and success!

Author of the best-selling
Murder In Amityville

DEATH OF A SCAVENGER
By Keith Spore

PRICE: $2.25   BT51465
CATEGORY: Mystery (Original)

Dr. Hugo Enclave takes on only the most clever
and cunning crimes, and is intrigued by those
considered unsolvable by the police. Enclave set
out to unravel the tangled threads surrounding the
death of Harland Rockmore, an investigator for a
law firm, whose body was found near his boss's
home after a scavenger hunt. Enclave moves
through a torturous labyrinth of murder, mayhem
and mystery to uncover a conspiracy aimed at
the White House itself!

THE KESSLER ALLIANCE
By Thomas Horstman

PRICE: $2.25   BT51463
CATEGORY: Novel (original)

A devastatingly prophetic novel of what could happen to the world, if Nazi extremists remained unchecked and their forces overthrew the world. Munich, Germany is the focal point of events and the birthplace of Wilhelm Kessler, a youth who becomes fascinated with Adolph Hitler. Another youth, Leo Maeder, becomes a Catholic priest. The lives of these two men become entwined as a bizarre series of events shake the world, and nations convulse under tremendous economic, political and social pressures. Only one man knew of the diabolical plot, but no one would believe him!

THE SEEING
By William P. McGivern
(Author of "Soldiers of '44,"
and "Night of the Juggler"
and Maureen McGivern

PRICE: $2.50 T51493
CATEGORY: Novel (Original)

THE SEEING is a contemporary occult thriller about
a child with profound psychic powers—whose gift
of prophecy becomes a force for evil!

"McGivern retains his stature as one of the very
best writers of suspense novels in the English lan-
guage."

—The Philadelphia Bulletir